ZOOMERS VS BOOMERS

ZOOMERS VS BOOMERS

SAWYER BLACK

STERLING & STONE

Copyright © 2022 by Sterling & Stone

All rights reserved.

No part of this book may be reproduced in any form or by any electronic or mechanical means, including information storage and retrieval systems, without written permission from the author, except for the use of brief quotations in a book review.

The authors greatly appreciate you taking the time to read our work. Please consider leaving a review wherever you bought the book, or telling your friends about it, to help us spread the word.

Thank you for supporting our work.

Chapter One

Craig's hand crept across his leg. Tapping fingers like a flesh-colored spider moving across the tight denim of his skinny jeans. Inches before it reached his phone in the center console, the spider balled up and retreated back to his lap.

He had promised his mother he wouldn't touch it for the entire drive, but the constant notifications were making it vibrate, almost jumping out of the cupholder. He flattened his shirt tail and crossed his arms with a sigh.

"That's awfully tight," his mother said.

"What?"

Her pale face was a mass of freckles attempting to congregate into one giant blotch across the bridge of her nose. Her hair — more gray than the ginger brown of her youth — blew around her in a wispy halo.

She looked like everybody else on her side of the family, while Craig looked just like his grandmother. Instead of tall and ethereal like his mother's people, he was shorter and darker like his father's. Craig was proud of his

Korean heritage, but he couldn't count the number of times somebody had asked him if he had been adopted.

Maybe if his father was still alive, there'd be less of a contrast between him and his mother. Two little white sisters with the family freckles didn't help. Slight Asian features and auburn hair, people said they looked "exotic."

No matter how offensive it was to describe somebody that way, it wasn't as bad as when he was described as *just* Asian.

"That shirt," his mother said. "It looks like body paint. And how many bracelets do you need?"

He could hear the smile in her voice, but he still felt the memory of criticism. A dust of fear still clinging to the old arguments.

His best friend had known long before he had dared tell anybody else. He told his sisters next.

Then his mother pointed to one of his more outlandish outfits. "Do you want people to think you're gay?"

He had thrown his hands out in frustration. "Mom! I *am* gay!"

She had fallen a step back as her hand rose to her throat in surprise. Then she nodded, as if finally figuring out the solution to a nagging problem. "*Ohhhh* … that makes sense."

And ever since that day, they had been good.

But how easy would life have been if he wasn't gay? Or if he didn't look so different? Or if his father hadn't gotten cancer just before Craig was born? Or if he didn't feel beholden to his followers, pressured to keep putting out content for them no matter how he was feeling?

As his phone continued to buzz and hum, Craig laced his fingers together in his lap. His mother was a great lady, and she deserved more from him than just his attention during the short drive to Jackson High. Like staying home and helping with the girls instead of spending a weekend with kids from school he could barely stomach on a good day.

But the ad revenue on his LiveLyfe channel, *Well Hyung Craig*, was enough to cover rent *and* the car payment. Soon, it would be enough for Mom to quit her job. Help pay for his college. Braces for Sarah and Samantha.

More bracelets for him!

He held his arm up, making the colorful arrangement flutter around his wrist. "I've also got my smartwatch on. Practicality is important."

"What's practical about it?"

"Mom." He pointed to the tiny screen. "It can track my sleep quality."

"And how is it?"

He shrugged. "Seems okay. I don't actually use it for that."

"Then what *do* you use it for?"

"I use it to change tracks on Spotify when I have my Bluetooth earbuds in. My pants are *way* too tight to keep pulling my phone out all the time."

She laughed so hard the Caravan swerved over to bounce along the rumble strips on the shoulder.

He'd come out to his followers right after the talk with his mother. Many people unsubscribed. Reported him to the LiveLyfe admins. Made videos of their own about how he was lying. Accusing him of clickbait for views. Saying he was trend chasing.

And the comments ...

Craig had been bullied at school before for being too small, for his slanted eyes, for his feminine traits even when he thought he'd done a good job of hiding them. The usual hazing that felt like a part of life. But some of what he read from those people had left him hollow for days.

Crying through his regret. Telling himself he should have stayed hidden.

Then the comments began to change.

He was strong. He was brave. He was an inspiration!

Over the last month of summer, his content changed to reflect the demands of his new audience — misfits like him who were trying to find their place amid the confusion — and he was suddenly ... "a hero."

Empowered by the empowerment he tried to convince his followers they had possessed all along. Convincing *himself* more than anyone else.

Then the last year of high school. A senior smaller than many incoming freshmen. Confidence the size of the moon.

New bullies. Some jealous because of his online fame. Some just because they hated "fags."

New friends. Some lured by his online fame. Some because they saw him for who he was. A young man forging ahead in spite of the dangerous waters.

But through it all, from the beginning, was Katherine. She was his best friend because she loved him no matter what. The same way his sisters loved him. Nobody was more happy for him than Kat when he finally came out. Her face had crumpled into tearful joy as she pulled him into her arms.

And then the first time he kissed a boy. Michael Hansen, a wiry frame topped by a rainbow mohawk. A wild two-week run that started as a glorious exploration of his freed sexuality. Ending in a sober talk about how he didn't like the way Michael used him as an identifier. Name-dropping and coattail-riding and more in love with the idea of Craig's minor celebrity than with Craig himself.

A head-spinning first semester. A new boyfriend every

two weeks. More money with every LiveLyfe statement. Grades slipping, then recovering. Even recognition from a few of the teachers.

Mr. Betz, his AP Calculus teacher, grabbed his shoulder. "You are doing your people proud."

Craig kept his voice smooth. Held himself still under the man's touch. "What do you mean, 'your people'?"

Mr. Betz shook his head in confusion. "Gay people."

And Craig realized Mr. Betz was right. *His* people. And they *were* proud of him. And he now had a responsibility to represent them.

The boy-chasing slowed down, and the chip on his shoulder — the one he hadn't even known he had carried — became a bit smaller.

He made a promise to his audience. "Here's how I make it through the tough times. I'll help you get through 'em, too."

Then he met Ira Odell.

Studious, nervous, and gorgeous. A geeky light-skinned Black kid that passed for white, resentful of how he was dismissed by both races. He had a successful LiveLyfe channel where he streamed speed runs of *Minecraft*. Something even Ira's own mother thought was a childish waste of time, in spite of his million followers that translated into thousands of dollars a month.

MINECRAFT, BUT EATING DROPS OP LOOT!

I BUILD AN UNDERWATER IRON FARM IN HARDCORE 1.18!

I SHOW WELL HYUNG CRAIG HOW TO PLAY MINECRAFT

. . .

CRAIG'S MOST successful collab to date. It spawned a series of videos that maintained high numbers. Earned him thousands of subscribers, his first true love, and his first real heartbreak.

It was right when KyMera had come to campus with their new wearable tech and their Operation: Gen Z contest.

Make a viral video. If it wins, you and the other streamers at your school get the chance to compete for a scholarship.

Craig got them into the final round without even trying. He streamed his prom. Went with Ira, dressed in a traditional Korean bridal dress. His mother had clasped her hands in front of her, staring at him through her tears. "Craig ... you are exquisite!"

That part of the video always got 'em.

Ira wore a tux with a cummerbund that matched Craig's dress. Held him to his side the entire night. But when it was over, and the cameras were finally turned off, Craig stood on his tiptoes to look into Ira's dark eyes. "I love you."

The words felt like electricity on his tongue.

Ira looked away with a nervous smile.

And then one word that hit like a gut punch.

"Thanks."

Craig didn't remember the rest of the night. Except for sobbing into his pillow, the thick mascara streaking into black stains that looked like the image burned into an ancient burial shroud.

He quietly broke up with Ira. Vowed he would put his audience first for a while, even as he took a break from streaming.

Marcy and Selena put them across the finish line. A series of makeup tutorials that ended with an hour-long process of helping a burn victim with her hair and makeup on her wedding day. Jessica Mendel. Caught in a car fire after a drunk driver hit her head-on. Her face was a puckered mess, and her hands were near useless nubs of flesh.

When Marcy and Selena were done, Jessica's face looked almost whole again. Craig remembered wiping his own tears away at the transformation.

KyMera had called a week later. Jackson High was the winner. Everybody seemed to forget it was his prom video that put them in the running while Marcy and Selena basked in the glow ... and Craig was fine with it.

Kat told him the people that mattered knew, but he had to admit that a video showcasing one of the worst nights of his life was better off overshadowed by something that ended in joy. Jessica Mendel and her dream wedding.

Craig smiled to himself. "What a year."

"What, sweetie?"

He pulled his gaze away from the blur of passing trees. "I don't know. It just feels like the days are ..."

"Flying by?"

"Kinda. More like they're shrinking. Like I don't have enough time for everything in my brain."

Her smile was wise. Almost smug. "It's going to get a whole lot worse."

"What will?"

"That feeling. Like you're always in a hurry and never catching up. Especially when you get to be my age. But you'll get a chance to slow down every now and again."

"Do you ever slow down?"

She pulled into the school parking lot. The bus from KyMera was already there. Bags piled beside it. Some of his fellow "influencers" saying their goodbyes.

"Not with you and your sisters running around like crazies all the time," she said.

Craig touched her arm as she pulled into a spot next to Jeff Roderick's Durango. "I was just thinking."

"About what, sweetie?"

Jeff walked around and leaned into the front window to give his mother a kiss on the cheek. He was a living sculpture of blond hair and muscle in his Jackson High Wildcats jersey. Then he returned to the rear window where his sister sat. She couldn't move much. Strapped to her giant motorized wheelchair. Just her head rocking and nodding on her slender neck. Her angelic smile.

Sweet and pretty and tragic.

"You know," Craig said. "Me being here at this dumb contest while you're alone with the girls. I could stay home and help you out."

"With what? It's not like they wear diapers anymore. Too young to date upperclassmen, and they know how to wash their own hoo-has."

"Oh, good Lord, Mom."

"I'm just saying, two thirteen-year-old girls are easier to handle than one seventeen-year-old Craig."

"Bullshit."

"And much like you, they aren't too old to put over my knee."

He held his hands up in defeat. "Okay, okay."

"Besides, if you win, you can afford to go to your school of choice."

"I get it, Mom. But that school will still have to want *me*."

She leaned over and grabbed his face between her hands. Pulled him in for a kiss. He couldn't help the giggles that burst out as their lips touched. He playfully swatted her hands away.

Jumped out as the giggles claimed her as well. Spun to

the back to get his backpack. "Thanks for embarrassing me, Mom."

"Hey!" she shouted, like she was letting the world know. "After you win this contest you can get your own car, and I won't embarrass you in public anymore."

"Okay, Jesus."

"Be safe. Have a great weekend! Call me when you can."

"Of course."

She made a kissy face. "I *wuvs* you, Cwaigs!"

He wouldn't let her leave without giving her what she wanted. He owed her so much for all that acceptance and support. He pitched his voice into a piercing falsetto. "I wuvs you too!"

She threw her head back with laughter as she pulled away. Her hand waving high out of the window. She was a tear-the-bandage-off-in-one-shot kind of gal. Get it over with and save the tears for later.

Craig turned away to face the other kids with a smile he hoped didn't look forced.

Chapter Two

Kat appeared at his side almost by magic. Craig's mother had barely left the parking lot when he felt her lean against him and give him a casual squeeze, her neck bent to rest her head on top of his.

He dropped his hand to her waist and turned with her to survey the other students standing amid piles of luggage. He only had a change of clothes, three clean pairs of underwear, and his hair gel. One backpack and whatever hung around his neck. Marcy and Selena had a mountain apiece. Selfie sticks. Vapid grins into the camera lenses.

He heard the whir of a drone. Looked up to shield his eyes as it fell to hover over the crowd.

It turned to follow Alexander "Oz" Hollins as he did a kicky flip thingy over a bench. Craig knew all the tricking and parkour moves had names of some kind — Hyper 360, Swipe Knife, Front Tuck, Butterfly Twist. He'd just never bothered to learn what went with what. Oz would happily sit him down and cover each one in detail. Along with a selection of videos depicting every one of his wipeouts.

Craig just honestly didn't care, though he wouldn't admit it out loud.

Oz was obsessed with Australia, had long hair that made many a girl jealous, and was confused about his identity. Caught between what he wanted and what his parents wanted for him, and Craig had long ago decided to support him in his quest to discover who he was. Unless that support included how to identify the differences between a Hypertwist and a Shuriken Twist.

Kat pulled her phone up, and Craig saw himself reflected on the screen. She had the camera set to mirror mode because she thought her face was asymmetrical, and seeing herself as others saw her made her uncomfortable. Craig thought she was beautiful, and was often as mystified as her when boys passed her up.

"What's up, guys! I'm here with Well Hyung Craig, just checking in."

It cracked him up to watch people fumble his channel name. People who didn't know what "hyung" actually meant. Only tripping over the word that felt Asian, but sounded dirty.

Kat had picked it up on her first try, and when Craig asked her why she didn't have a problem with it, she'd looked at him like he'd asked why the sky was blue.

"I love EXO Group."

He had shaken his head in confusion.

"K-pop?"

He shrugged.

"They're a South Korean boy band."

"And that's how you know that *hyung* means 'big brother'?"

"Yep."

Best friends ever since.

After spinning him around to give her followers a view

of the parking lot where the other kids were doing much the same, she signed off with her usual, "See you later, guys!"

Malcolm Cook whizzed by on his Onewheel electric skateboard. The mind of a brain-damaged juvenile stunt performer over the body of a marble statue, he was Jeff's buddy. Craig suspected it wasn't out of any genuine friendship, so much as sharing a water polo team and both having carved abs that drove the views up on their respective LiveLyfe channels.

Jeff threw up his hand without looking. Malcolm's high-five landed like their palms were made of magnets.

Craig didn't envy their looks. The muscles and the hair. The perfect skin that naturally bronzed in the summer. Straight teeth and hairless, streamlined legs.

Not much, anyway.

He *really* envied their casual physicality. How cool it was to just stick up your hand and have a high-five like it was meant to be there all along? Or to look good in every single outfit, even when you were slumming it? The attitude of appearing not to care, because they didn't. When everything looked good on you, why pay attention?

If you did it only *drew* attention. The wrong kind.

Jeff had never bullied him, but Malcolm was often there with an errant elbow. A snicker and a pointing finger. Clever put-downs that proved he had a quicker wit than his grades might suggest.

"I can't believe their channels have the views to get them into this," Craig said, barely avoiding a sarcastic sneer. "A bunch of teenage girls slobbering on the tops of their fur-lined boots, hoping for a glimpse of his shaved chest."

Kat blushed as she looked away.

Craig choked back his laughter. "Wait. Are *you* one of those girls?"

Her jaw firmed as she looked back. "Yes, I am. But I also subscribe to *your* channel, and you shave your chest too."

Craig pointed at Jeff's back. "He shaves his chest. I just don't have much hair. Naturally dolphin smooth."

She laughed. "Wow, thanks for putting that image in my head. Can you do a dolphin noise?"

"Only in bed," he teased.

"Wow," she said, rubbing her eyes. "I really need to bleach that from my mind."

Before he could think of a witty comeback to keep the jokes going, Ira stepped into their huddle. "Did you guys see my *GTA V* video I posted this morning?"

His usual smile seemed tired. Puffy eyes and shadows under his gaunt cheekbones. Craig grabbed his wrist and looked up with concern. "Were you editing all night?"

Ira reached up and rubbed Craig's shoulder. Still good friends after the prom disaster, even though Ira's touch still sent a thrill through him. "Yeah, but it was a banger. Had to give the channel one more before the weekend."

"Won't you be streaming most of this, though?"

Ira shrugged. "It's not the same thing. My viewers want gaming content. They don't really care about the BTS stuff."

Kat didn't have to push up on her toes to hug him. They were the same height, and Craig was standing in their combined shadow. "What did you do?" she asked.

Craig was suddenly struck by how grown-up he suddenly felt when Ira returned Kat's embrace with a kiss on the cheek. "I escaped five stars in an ambulance."

Craig sighed. "I don't know what that means."

Kat smiled down at him before returning her attention

to Ira. "I think you're wrong. If you look at your comments, you'll see a lot of people want the behind-the-scenes videos."

Craig pulled them apart. "Seriously, I don't know what that five star thing is."

Ira shrugged as he met Craig's gaze. "My fans still ask about you."

Craig kept his face still. Just a small smile of interest. "Do they?"

A new voice distracted him from his question as Mia Wu skipped up to bounce off of Craig's hip. "Is that shirt tight enough, Craigers?"

She looked like one of her Gacha Life characters. Anime makeup and pink ponytails. Schoolgirl outfit that would certainly drive her views up.

Craig had often wondered how many of her subscribers were dirty old men watching her streams to get a look at her low tops, but if he mentioned it to her, Mia would only stare back in confusion. She dressed that way because she liked it, seemingly unaware of its effect. Though she couldn't be completely oblivious, as her videos and Discord were often flooded with lecherous comments.

"It's as tight as your skirt is short."

She grinned, batting her heavy eyelashes. "Then it's perfect."

Ira pointed over Craig's shoulder. "Is that the bus?"

Craig turned to look at the giant OPERATION: GEN Z graphic plastered under the KyMera logo. He looked back at Ira with a frustrated shrug. "I don't know. If only there was some kind of clue."

Kat nodded in agreement. "Yeah, like, I dunno, a sign or something."

Mia laughed as she dropped her bags in line with the

rest. "This where it all goes? Like, will somebody load it for us?"

While Ira rolled his eyes, Craig followed Mia to drop his backpack next to hers. She looked him up and down in confusion. "Why aren't you making a video?"

"Just taking a break, ya know? Besides, I'll be streaming during the contest, whatever it is."

"Yeah, does anybody know what it is yet?"

"Nope. Besides, I'm in enough of everybody else's videos to slake the thirst of my audience."

She grabbed his hand as they walked back to their friends. "Ooh, *slake*. That's a fun word."

Craig nodded. "Yeah, for some reason it sounds dirty."

Mia's squealing laughter brought attention. She was almost his exact size, making it difficult for him to hide behind her. She was a tiny force of nature, dragging him into the light no matter how hard he tried to avoid it.

He had no choice but to go along with it, but was saved the effort when the bus door popped open with a clanging hiss.

The bus rocked with the driver's weight as he tromped down the stairs. Clomping footsteps. Thick hands holding the door to the side as he stepped into the sun.

He looked like he had filled up the entire interior. Gray hair gone to white at the temples, swept to the side from the hard part razored into his scalp. Neat goatee trimmed to reveal the hard angles of his jaw. Thick neck that led to powerful shoulders under a tight black T-shirt. KyMera logo stretched across his broad chest. Jeans cut loose for the sand-colored boots.

"Afternoon!" Grinning with perfect teeth as he waved and stepped aside.

"*He's* a silver fox," Craig breathed.

Kat shrugged. "I guess."

"Okay, kids. Let's say we start getting on board."

Malcolm snorted. "*Kids?*"

The driver flapped his hand in a dismissive apology. "Sorry about that. You get to a certain age, and *everybody's* a kid."

Even straightening to his full height, Malcolm wasn't as tall as the driver. Nor as thick. Craig wondered if Malcolm was aware of the size difference. Or the way the driver was standing. Where Malcolm looked like he was trying to look big, the driver just was. Relaxed but *ready*. Ex-military. Or just a guy who knew how to handle himself. The kinda guy Craig bet never got picked on as a kid, never had to pretend to be more manly than he felt.

"That's cool, Grandpa," Malcolm said.

The driver's smile slipped. Eyes narrowed, and a muscle in his jaw bulged. "The name's Ray. I'll be driving you to the site as soon as the rest of you show up."

Jeff stepped forward next to Malcolm's false confidence. "Only one of you?"

Ray shrugged. "There's only *twelve* of you. I think I can handle a dozen kids."

Craig noticed the cameras and phones pointed at Ray. Saw his smile recover. Realized he was aware of the cameras too.

Mia pulled on Craig's arm. "I agree with you," she whispered in his ear. "He's pretty hot for an old guy."

Ray pointed to the pile of bags next to the bus. "You can leave everything here. It'll be my pleasure to take care of it for you."

"What about Karen?" Marcy said.

Ray turned his gaze to where Marcy stood next to Selena, but it was clear he didn't know which one had spoken. "Miss Beal will be at the site to onboard you. In the meantime, you can sit inside in the AC. Go through the goody bag we left you."

Oz was walking before Ray had finished talking. "Goody bags? Heck yeah!"

He brought his fist up as he neared the door, and Craig almost burst into laughter when Ray looked at it like it was a swollen maggot hanging in the air. But then his grin was right back as he brought his own hand up for a fist bump as Oz jumped inside.

It was like the signal everybody was waiting for.

Malcom ignored Ray on his way inside, but Craig was surprised to hear Marcy and Selena both thank him on their way by.

He counted nine of them as he filed toward the door. Looked over his shoulder as more cars pulled in, but stopped when he saw Jeff lean in and touch his sister's cheek. She giggled, her head rolling with her emotion.

The Range Rover pulled away, and Jeff sighed before turning toward the bus.

It looked like he didn't want to be here. Curious ...

Craig spun back before he could get caught staring. He nodded to Ray as he jumped up the steps into a cool wash of interior air. Ray nodded back, and Craig noticed his friendly grin wasn't in his eyes.

Cold and pale.

Like Jeff, it looked like Ray didn't want to be here, either.

Chapter Three

Walking into the bus made Craig want to put his hands in his pockets. Tile that looked like marble. Wooden trim polished to shine so much it was like he could reach right into it. Leather that looked like melting butter.

He would surely soil whatever he touched.

Malcolm flopped into one of the overstuffed seats like it was an old couch in the basement. Marcy and Selena sat on opposite ends of a loveseat lounger with their feet drawn up beneath them. Both with their shoes still on.

There was enough room on the bus for a hundred people — if they were packed in like the public transit the less fortunate suffered. With the thick cushions and open spaces, there was just enough for the twelve of them.

A small kitchen with a wide sink and full-sized refrigerator. A small bathroom with shiny fixtures peeking through the open door.

Craig sat on one side of a loveseat in the back. Pressed into the corner with his knees pulled together. Hands flat on his thighs. Kat dropped down next to him.

"This is the nicest bus I've ever seen."

Ira pulled Mia into the plush leather across the aisle. "It's just about the nicest *anything* I've ever seen."

Mia lifted a small bag from the cushion before settling in. "I almost sat on the goodies."

Craig felt around on either side of him, careful to keep his skin from dragging across the leather. A soft bag held by a gold drawstring. He got the image of a bottle of whiskey. Couldn't think of the brand he was reminded of.

"Ooh, a cold brew with sweet cream," Mia squealed.

Kat rolled her eyes. "Yeah, but it's from Hill of Beans."

Mia's face became offended and pouty. "But I *like* Hill of Beans."

Ira snorted laughter. "Liking something doesn't mean it's good."

"I like you too, so what does *that* say?"

Ira cracked open the bottle. Paused before taking a sip. "Means I'm better than Hill of Beans."

"That doesn't make any sense."

Craig ignored them to look into his own bag. Glass bottle of sweet coffee made to look like it catered to the refined tastes of discerning coffee lovers the world over when he knew it was made on an assembly line by minimum wage chemists. Pumpkin spice hand sanitizer. Wireless earbuds that actually looked decent. KyMera's stylized flame logo stamped on the case. A paracord bracelet — orange and black to match Jackson High's school colors — with a small KyMera charm hanging from the clasp.

He snapped it on without thinking, pausing for a moment to admire it sliding over the rest. Dug back into the bag for the last goody. A bag of Sour Patch Kids.

"First they're sweet," Mia sang.

Kat pushed into Craig's shoulder. "Then they're sour."

He could already smell the fruity sugar filling the air.

He cinched the drawstring and leaned back. Kat squeezed his knee. "What's a matter?"

Craig felt the bus shift as somebody boarded. Looked up to see Ty Hawkins bop on with his usual thousand-watt smile. Hand up to catch Jeff with a high five. Other hand full of phone as he streamed to his followers.

The contrast of his teeth against his skin — almost as black as charred paper and as smooth as polished glass — was practically a trademark. Probably why he smiled so much.

He was in the "lifestyle influencer" category, but he preferred to call himself a "life guide." Helping other young Black men live their best while looking their best. His most viral video was a confrontation with a man in line at American Eagle.

It turned racist, but Ty maintained a calm that made him seem so much older and wiser than he was. A disposition that infected the crowd. That crept into the other man's soul until he ended up apologizing. Shook his hand. Then an embrace.

Craig thought that smile had something to do with it. Disarming and beautiful, Craig was sure it would be the thing Ty was famous for one day. On every magazine cover. Commercials. Maybe even movies.

Craig glanced over to Kat's concern. "Nothing. Just … I don't know. I just feel like I don't belong here."

Kat popped another piece of candy in her mouth as she shook her head. "It was your video that got us into the finals."

Ira looked up from his bag. They had eventually talked after that night. Ira hadn't been ready to love, let alone *say* it. But when he *was* ready to love, he hoped to find somebody like Craig.

Craig shook his head. "It was Selena and Marcy that put us over."

"Oh my God," Mia squeaked. "He's sweating already." She stared at the front of the bus with a Sour Patch Kid poised in front of her parted lips.

Craig followed her gaze to see Kelly Smalls walk down the aisle with his skateboard under his arm. Drawn in like he was trying to make himself ... smaller.

He hung out with Oz. Parkour and skateboarding. Two bros just loving the outdoors, but his online fame was from live drawing *Dragon Ball Z* characters.

Intricate details and dynamic composition in twenty minutes. His entry was an hour-long livestream of a detailed drawing of Goku and Chi-Chi standing with their sons Gohan and Goten, all of them looking ready to kick ass.

He could have been one of the most popular kids in school, if not for his sweating problem. Emotional moisture that slicked his face and hands. His friendship with Oz helped keep the bullies at bay, but it still earned him the nickname, Kelly *Smells*.

As he flopped down onto the soft leather next to Oz, the last kid jumped on. Thick black coils hanging over her face. Her hand holding her phone up to her ear under the fall of her afro. Huge sunglasses. Tight black outfit that looked like military fatigues. Heavy boots a motorcyclist would wear. A stark contrast to her usual glamorous over-achieving look. Alicia Brown.

She dropped into the first seat. Curled up around her conversation, turning away from the rest of them.

Craig sniffed as he turned back to his friends and crossed his legs. "Stuck-up bitch."

Kat slapped his shoulder. "Craig!"

Mia tipped her head back to pour the loose sugar from

the bag's floor into her mouth. Crinkled the empty bag into her tiny fist. Smacked her lips. "He's right though. Little Miss Rich Head Cheerleader. Perfect in every way, except she's failing history."

Ira chuckled. "How do you fail history? It already happened."

Craig was certain her videos were only popular because she tended to show a lot of skin. Casually bending over in skirts and stuff, like she didn't know she was being watched. Every inch of skin was just a byproduct of her self-acceptance. Maybe he wouldn't despise her so much if she wasn't a stuck-up princess who wouldn't give the time of day to anyone not in her clique.

The money bothered him too. Not just that she was stinking rich and flaunted it often, but her father bought LiveLyfe ads and followers. Everything about her felt manufactured for views. A video about her sitting next to her pool in a tiny bikini "studying" for finals? Pursing her lips to hold the pen in her mouth.

His mother had sighed at his complaint. "Why do you care what a girl does with her body?"

"What?"

"She's free to do whatever she wants. Real money, or this social currency you're always talking about. How can you be pro sex workers and feminism yet be so judgmental of her?"

"I don't know why it bothers me so much. Why can't she do something else? Something real that requires thoughts or personality?"

His mother had countered, "Maybe she's like you, keeping her true self a secret because this is the version of her that people accept?"

"I don't think she's that deep, Mom."

"Even if she's not deep, who are *you* to judge? If you were smoking hot, what would *you* do?"

He had cocked his hip out. "I *have* a smoking hot body. I just don't have the money. I guess I'll have to cure cancer or something."

They had laughed, but still it bothered him. And the fact that it bothered him made it worse. He didn't *want to* be a judgmental asshole like so many of the sexist guys who gave girls on the internet shit just for existing or making money off their looks.

"I just think she can do better." Craig sounded like the asshole he didn't think he was.

Kat rolled her eyes as she threw herself back into her cushion. "Better than *what*? Being the hottest girl at school?"

"At school?" Ira said. "How about the town?"

Mia spread her hands. "The whole state."

Craig waved them away. "I get it, I get it." He didn't want to look into why it bothered him anymore. That uncomfortable feeling he got when she shamelessly bent over in front of the camera. Imagining a breathless boy staring at the screen.

The bus began to roll, and Kat fell against him with a surprised giggle. Craig caught her as if he was saving her from falling to the floor. Joined in with her laughter. Pushed his ... jealousy? resentment? aside, telling himself not to worry about Alicia Brown.

"Hey!" Jeff shouted. "What about our bags?"

Craig hopped up to spin on his knee. Looked out the window as the pile of bags slid by, still on the ground where they'd left them. He felt his friends press in against him.

"I'm just a driver." His voice sounded easy. Like he was

on the verge of laughing. "There's a guy coming in a truck to get the bags. He'll be along shortly."

Jeff stood and spread his hands. "There's not enough room on this thing?"

"I'm not an engineer, either." Ray shrugged. "Karen Beal told me to do what I'm doing, and that's what you get."

"Karen Beal?" Selena said, her hand going up to cover her mouth.

"Yes, ma'am. The head of KyMera herself. Waiting to welcome you in person when we get to Oakridge."

An excited silence settled over them. Just the creaking of leather. The rise of the engine as the bus hit the highway.

Karen Beal was like Elon Musk by way of Dolly Parton. The sweetest, most down-home Southern lady in the world, mixed with the mind of a tech engineering giant. Proper manners over ruthless business. She had as many followers of her fashion channel as she did of her industry videos.

Craig had watched an hour of her talking to the camera about peach pie recipes while a robot Beal had built when she was just seventeen painted her nails.

Noise on the bus grew as the phones came back out. He felt it in his pocket. Vibration from the incoming notifications. He tapped the face of his watch. Swiped down and put it in Goodnight Mode. The vibrations stopped.

He closed his eyes and thought about his followers watching him meet a famous person. Watching him break up with his love on prom night. Watching him lounge around the pool in a tight pair of trunks.

His mother would laugh at him, but Craig just didn't feel like being watched right now.

Chapter Four

"Man, Malcolm's about to start a livestream," Kat said from her spot beside him, smiling as she stared at her phone, knowing that Craig hated Malcolm's persona even more on video than in person.

A teaser was counting down the minutes to the livestream.

Craig pulled up Malcolm's LiveLyfe channel and sighed as he scrolled past the placeholder video and read several clickbait titles with little value other than their unintentional comedy. "Please tell me you don't enjoy this."

"I *enjoy* watching the look of pain on your face," she teased.

He started reading titles, his voice low, lest Malcolm overhear him from a few seats away.

"24 HOURS IN A PIZZA PIRATE."

"COOKING WITH TIKTOK LIFE HACKS."

"MY NEW SILVERADO — CRASHED IMMEDIATELY."

"THE THREE PIZZA CHALLENGE."
"MY GIRLFRIEND CAUGHT ME CHEATING!!"

"GOD, SUCH LOW-HANGING FRUIT," Craig said.

"Yeah, but his audience eats it up. Check out his Patreon page."

Craig clicked over and laughed at the tiers, ranging from two dollars a month — "That's less than a fucking latte double shot, guys" — to get behind-the-scenes footage and "special premiere privileges," all the way up to fifty dollars which got you a T-shirt with his catchphrase silkscreened on the chest.

STAY OUT OF THE KITCHEN.

"OH, LOOK, TOP TIER GETS 'A CHANCE' to have a one-on-one call with the legend himself!" Kat could barely get the words out without laughing.

"I can't imagine a world where someone, let alone many someones, spends fifty bucks a month on Malcom crap, or the opportunity to have a one-on-one with him. God, imagine the conversations!"

"Well, I think you're ignoring the scientific importance here. How else, short of a time machine, would scientists get a chance to see how Neanderthals communicated with one another?"

Craig laughed as he read the copy. "*Come and join thousands of other Malcomtents!* Good God, I'm not sure what's worse, that kids would willingly fork over money to him every month or willingly call themselves such a stupid name."

"Go back, go back, it's about to start," Kat said with *way* too much enthusiasm.

He clicked back. The chat window was flooded with rapid-fire comments coming in from his fans, so fast it was hard to catch more than a bit of one or another before it was gone.

"So many live viewers for ... this shit?" Craig sighed.

SANJAY MENARD — hi
 Big G Monee — HAVE SOME CHEESE
 Small_thickboy — just 1 more minute
 Mike Mike — NOOOOOOOO I gotta go to class
 Sanjay Menard — I have a bag of funions and a 2 liter of dr pepper plus a box of zebra cakes ... and a paintbrush for some reason
 Pablo Guy — In my country, it's night.
 Tom Mathews — how are you
 Fosu foster — I'm in the shower so I can poop at the same time
 Sanjay Menard — soon
 BobGaming — this is gonna be amazing
 Willie Biggun — my dad left and I'm sad I mean I'm fine :)
 Be kind — woooooooooooooooooooooooooooo
 Sanjay Menard — 30 seconds
 Burrito YES — poggers
 Be kind — start

THE VIDEO FEED WENT LIVE. Immediately Malcolm's face in the bus seat filled the screen.

Malcolm raised the phone to his face and used the screen as a mirror. Adjusted his hair. Then straightened in mock surprise as if he just now noticed his followers watching him.

"Oh, hey there, Malcolmtents. It's your boy, Malcom Cook. Let's watch what he Coox today!" Yes, he actually referred to himself in the third person. "And, remember, if you can't stand the smoke—"

Malcolm then took a deep breath as he stared into the camera like he was the preacher at a wedding waiting for somebody to speak now ... or forever hold their peace.

"—then stay out of the kitchen."

MOUSE RODRIGUEZ — its about time
    James gun — sup
    Sanjay Menard — yeah boi!!!!!

MALCOLM SPUN the camera around and thrust it into Jeff's face. "My dude, Jeff is hangin' with me." Then he turned the camera to take a sweeping view of the luxury of the bus. "Your boy is riding in style! Look at this bitch."

    Harley Jenkins — big pimping
    MackSupreme — can I get an ohhh yeah!

MALCOLM LOWERED the camera to show the rest of the Jackson High kids. "On our way to the ... Oak Limb Academy? Whatever it's called. The *thing*! Right? Gonna be Karen Beal herself there. Pretty hype."

SANJAY MENARD — our beal and savior
    Aminsherd — what's the big beal? I mean DEAL?
    Brad brad jr — it's my birthday

Javon Leroy — leather leather leather
Brandon Parks — daddy chill

MALCOLM PAUSED on Kelly's skateboard and scanned up as Kelly crossed his arms and looked away, his face dripping. "Looks like Smells is already wet. Must be from being so close to me."

Kelly lowered his own phone to pause his stream. "Come on, man. It's hot in here."

Malcolm spun the camera to fill the screen with his own beaming face. "It's *not* hot in here. Well, maybe in another seat." He turned the view to focus on Selena and Marcy, snuggled together to talk to their followers. Heads touching, just like their phones. Selena arched an eyebrow. Glanced up and extended her middle finger.

Malcolm laughed. "Sorry, ladies, my butt is exit only, but maybe our boy Craig would take you up on—" The camera spun to show Craig looking up awkwardly from his phone, as if he hadn't been caught watching Malcolm's stream. He too extended a middle finger.

The camera then turned to Kat, shoving a handful of Sour Patch Kids into her mouth.

"Ooh." Jeff bounded towards them. "Can I have some?"

"Sorry," Kat said, opening her mouth to reveal the colorful wad of candy. "All gone."

Malcolm put the camera in Craig's face as Craig turned his phone over.

Malcolm smiled. "So, what were you watching? You a closet Malcomtent?"

"Actually, yes. Wanna join me? Plenty of room in my closet." He winked at Malcolm, extra-gay.

Kat and Mia laughed.

"Fucking gross," Malcolm muttered in flight from the laughter.

His camera caught Jeff trying not to smile. Malcolm dropped down next to him, camera in his face.

"Fuck *off*," Jeff said, though more with a grin than any actual anger.

Malcolm turned the camera to settle on Ray's wide shoulders. "Our bus driver looks like Wolverine's grandpa. He ain't all that, though."

Jeff reached into view to poke Malcolm in the ribs.

Malcolm jumped with a yelp.

"How do you know he ain't all that?" Jeff asked.

Malcolm rubbed the spot with a wince. "I can just tell."

Jeff rolled his eyes. Smiled as he shook his head. "Whatever, man."

Malcolm held the phone out to capture them both in the frame. "You wanna say something to the Malcolmtents?"

Jeff shook his head. "Nah, I gotta finish editing yesterday's video to re-post. *Somebody* said something *really* wrong in that one, and LiveLyfe tried to demonetize it."

Malcolm stared into the camera with a guilty smile. "Yeah, uh ... sorry about that, bro."

"Yeah, well ... it was the one where we put the treads on Angel's wheelchair so she could go down to the shore with us. I had to bleep your nonsense out."

Malcolm shrugged. "I gotta be me, you know? But with that being said, go to my dude's channel. Superslick Roderick. Subscribe and click notifications so you never miss a video, and check out what we did to Angel's wheelchair. Hit it with a like."

He brought up his hand in a devil horns. Snarled with his tongue out. "Cooking more later. I'll send a message out before I go live again. *Peace!*"

The video cut off to a black rectangle.

SANJAY MENARD — poggers
　Triston97 — I hope he wins
　RayWade — who's angel?

JEFF'S LIVELYFE channel was far more subdued than Malcolm's. Titles with less clickbait.

MY BIRTHDAY AT THE LAKE WITH ANGEL
　WE WON THE BIG GAME — ANGEL THE CHEERLEADER
　ANGEL IS BACK FROM THE HOSPITAL
　MY SISTER THINKS I'M FUNNY

FEWER FOLLOWERS THAN MALCOLM, but more views per video. Especially the videos about his sister. Her sweet smile was a guarantee. More clicks than when he threw the winning touchdown. Her laugh alone was almost enough to turn a video viral.

There were no stupid catchphrases. No Patreon links. No merchandise. Just a donation link to the Cerebral Palsy Foundation.

His most popular video was the one where he took Angel to his senior prom. Guiding her to the dance floor, her face shining in joy. His girlfriend looking on with tears in her eyes as he moved around Angel's chair. Craig's sweeping gown in the background.

It was the featured video on his LiveLyfe page. The one that introduced potential followers to the kind of content they could expect. The one that helped push Jackson High's numbers over the top. A video about the love a boy had for his sister.

Chapter Five

Craig leaned back after Malcolm went away. Intent on ignoring everything around him. The sudden noise of everyone talking in unison. The LiveLyfe influencer bullshit.

He felt dirty sitting in the bright luxury of the bus. A spot in a contest just because he did something a stranger thought was *Worthy*. Of what?

He had no idea.

IT SEEMED like he had barely closed his eyes when Kat jabbed him in the ribs. His back ached, and a line of sweat across his chest cooled as he lowered his arms. His fingers were numb.

"What?"

Kat giggled. "Ray just told us we're here."

Craig blinked the sleep from his eyes. Shook his head. "Here where?"

Ira leaned forward to rest his elbows on his knees. "You were snoring."

Mia pointed out the window. "We're at Oakridge."

Craig squinted through the glass, but he saw only a tall chain-link fence with branches hanging over the top. Black algae clinging to the metal posts. "Does it get better?"

Mia's face pinched into confusion. "Better than what? We just got here."

The bus slid along the fence. Slowing as it neared. Craig anticipated contact, but Ray was a better driver than he imagined, and the bus came to a gentle stop with the door in line with a break in the fence. An open gate. Beyond it, woods, and a giant, decrepit old building.

Craig looked at all the other kids. Their faces full of excitement and curiosity. A blush of fear.

"Oh man!" Malcolm cried.

Craig's heart leapt into his throat at the sound. He swallowed the pounding back down.

Malcolm pointed to his phone. "There's no signal."

Oz pulled his knit beanie off and ran his fingers through his hair. "Doesn't look good for a tech company, huh?"

"Yeah," Ira agreed. "How are we supposed to stream the contest? Or *anything*?"

Ray opened the door, and the bus bounced under the steps of somebody coming in. Craig wanted to see who it was. But he also wanted to look away. He wondered if it was just his bad mood. Wishing he could just be home with the girls. Eating popcorn and watching *Frozen* for the thousandth time.

"There *is* a signal," Karen Beal said, mounting the top step and moving into the aisle. "Just not for *those* devices." Her voice was soft and pleasant. Warm and polite.

She was pale. Soft business suit. The pointed toes of sand cowgirl boots poked out of the perfect fall of her pant legs. Dangling earrings that jangled like spurs when she moved. She was barely taller than Mia, but it felt like she filled the whole bus. Ray stood up behind her, and it was like a cloud passing over the sun.

When they all just stared at her in silence, she grinned. Clapped her hands in front of her like she was delighted to see them. Her nails were impractically long. Red and glittering.

"Children, this is more than a contest. To be frank, it is also a beta."

"Beta? Got a couple beta cucks here." Malcolm winked at Craig.

Craig turned away, shaking his head.

Karen lifted her head. "Not that kind of beta, Mr. Cook. A beta *test*."

Ira grunted a soft whisper of breath. "Figures."

"What figures, Mr. Odell?"

Ira straightened like he had been called on in school. "Um ... nothing."

"Oh, come now. We're all friends here."

Craig saw Ray's snarl before ducking his head.

Ira spread his hands. His mouth opened and closed. Opened again. "I just ... that's just the way it always works, right? They say it's one thing, but then it turns out to be another."

Karen lifted one eyebrow. "*They?*"

"Yeah. Like game makers and phone manufacturers. Movie trailers, even."

She nodded. "I understand. It might feel like a social betrayal of sorts. But the reality is that I sponsor the contest. I make the wearable tech you will use during your time here. I have personally developed and paid for the new wireless network being used to stream the massive amounts of video, audio, GPS, and telemetry data required for the next generation of communications systems, and if I choose to leverage this contest into reviewable and actionable numbers, as well as a measure of publicity for my company ... and you and your school ... should I, or *they*, not be entitled?"

Ira looked around for support. Saw none forthcoming. Shrugged. "Yes? I mean, no! Or ..." He trailed off, lowering his gaze to the floor.

Karen laughed. An easy sound without malice, and Craig relaxed the grip he didn't know had been digging his fingers into the cushion next to him.

Karen clapped her hands again. "And it begins now."

Confused faces. Craig saw his alarm reflected back at him. He'd just woken up. And he needed to pee. He darted into the small restroom in the back. Closed the door on the protesting voices behind him.

He turned the water on. Stepped to the toilet. Marveled for a moment at how the restroom looked like one he would have seen in a nice house instead of a nice bus. Shivered so hard his stream almost shot over the edge.

The water was steaming when he finished. After washing his hands, he splashed a little on his face. Used the soft towel that was already damp from the last person. He wondered if it had been Jeff or Malcolm.

He almost washed his hands and face again.

Instead, he drew a deep breath and walked into the awkwardness of being the center of attention. Every gaze fixed on him. Including Karen's. Ray glaring at him over his shoulder.

Craig swallowed. "Sorry."

Karen's grin came back, and she waved his apology away. "Quite alright, Mr. Boucher. This was all I had on my schedule for today. My momma always told me about the importance of leisure time, and I do not want to put her to shame."

Craig wasn't sure what that meant, but by the looks on the other faces, he wasn't sure the underlying sentiment was even true. He wondered what she had said about him while he'd been in the restroom. He sat back down with a growing distrust chewing at his belly.

An uneasy sweat broke out on the back of his neck.

Karen waited until he was settled before continuing. Thankfully, the sound of her voice brought the attention away from him as everybody looked back to the front. "Now then. You will leave your devices on the bus."

A low-grade grumble nearly swelled into a full complaint, but when she held up one hand, the silence resumed. Craig felt like it was more fearful than respectful.

He no longer felt the shared excitement. It was more like dread.

Karen reached up to touch her hair. Like she was making sure it was still there. "You will then leave my bus. Outside, Ray here will assign to you the wearable devices you'll use for the duration."

Malcolm pushed forward to the edge of his seat. "The duration of what?"

Karen didn't look at him. "Why, the duration of the contest, Mr. Cook."

Kelly jumped up. "Really?" Craig expected Karen to rip into him, but then he realized Kelly was looking at Malcolm. "This is Karen Beal. The owner of one of the biggest tech firms in America. KyMera is into global satellite internet. One of the most-used operating systems in automated manufacturing. Robotics technology decades ahead of Japan. Data delivery systems that make streaming video to more simultaneous users that almost *everybody* uses. Including all of our LiveLyfe channels. I mean …" He suddenly realized that everybody was staring at him. His red face dripping sweat.

He sat down like his knees had been kicked from behind. "Why would she want to steal our stuff? Just do it. Why else are we here?"

Karen inclined her head. "Thank you, Mr. Smalls."

Mia pointed a trembling finger to the front of the bus. "And that suit is lovely."

Karen laughed again, draining the tension yet again. "And thank *you*, Miss Wu."

Kat leaned into Craig to whisper, "She knows all of our names?"

Karen clasped her hands in front of her chest. "Please. Any device that can transmit or receive data — leave it in your seat. We will not bother any of them. Phones. Watches. Drones, Mr. Hollins. Wireless cameras. Once you leave the bus, you will receive the absolute latest KyMera has to offer. You won't be disappointed."

No grumbling this time. Only compliance as they stood to remove their devices and put them in the seats behind them.

Craig wanted to take a quick look to see if he had gotten any texts while asleep, but Karen shouted, "Come along, children. Outside with Mr. Wardell, please. We will get you outfitted, go over the rules, and get underway. My momma told me there was no better way to do something than getting to it."

"Ain't nothing to it but to do it," Ty said, his smile like a beacon.

Her smile couldn't match his radiance, but it was close. "Exactly so, Mr. Hawkins."

Craig shuffled into the line leaving the bus. No talking. Just scraping feet and excited breathing. He resisted the urge to pull away from Karen as he passed her. Like she would burn him if he got too close.

Ray was standing outside, watching the kids go by,

through a gate to a row of red bags. Each had the KyMera name sewn into it. Something else stitched below it. When he got closer, Craig saw it was a name. Each had their own bag.

He looked up at an ancient wooden sign, its painted letters cracked and faded.

OAKRIDGE ACADEMY.

MORE MOSS AND algae than paint, but the words were still legible.

Behind it, rising like a monolith that refused to stay buried, was a crumbling building. Dark holes for windows. Creeping ivy yanking bricks from the walls. An overgrown path narrowed to the front doors of peeling green paint.

An old school. Now decaying in the setting sun.

"The rules are simple, children." Karen stood on the ground in front of the bus steps. Another woman stepped into view through the gate opening. She leaned in to whisper into Karen's ear. Karen nodded before continuing. "Overcome the obstacle courses and reach the tap point in the auditorium. Touch your new phones to the signal plate for the win. The prize is a million dollars set to deposit directly in a crypto account tied to the phone. Two people can win together and split the entire pot. Three or more means the money is forfeit, and the contest is over."

Ray turned to grab the gate. As he swung it shut, Alicia stood with her bag slung over her shoulder. "What are the other rules?"

The gate slammed shut, and Ray turned with a smile as he locked it behind him.

"There are no other rules," Karen shouted as she ascended the steps and the door slid shut.

The engine fired up with a soft growl. As the bus pulled away, Ray turned on his heel and stomped off.

Ty threw his hands up. "The fuck is he going?"

Ray disappeared into the thick bushes on the other side of the fence. Craig noticed he hardly made any noise passing through the leaves and branches.

Selena put one hand on her hip. Pointed with the other one. "The fuck is *she* going?"

Alicia Brown was walking away, toward woods near the fence, away from the gate. Her heels striking off the broken concrete with a purpose. Head down. Arms swinging.

Malcolm turned in a slow circle. "The fuck is going on?"

Craig felt the hair on the back of his neck stand up. Smelled burning ozone. Heard the spitting of electricity over his head. He looked up. Traced the heavy electrical lines overhead.

From a pole in the distance, dropping down to the fence behind them.

He edged away from it. Dropped to the ground next to the bag with his name on it.

"Holy shit," Ira said.

Craig looked over to see him pull a new phone out of the bag.

"It's the KyMera AT10. This isn't supposed to come out for like two more years."

Craig reached into his own bag. Pulled the shiny device out. No buttons. Just a small gold diamond of metal on the side. He ran his thumb along it, and the phone screen brightened.

It resolved into his LiveLyfe profile picture.

He was already logged into it.

His profile disappeared to reveal a pair of icons. His LiveLyfe streaming button, and KyMera's Gen Z button.

He pushed the latter, and the screen changed to show an isometric view of the Oakridge Academy grounds. Red glowing dots showing the location of the other kids. A green one showing him where he sat in front of the closed gate. A glowing flash of gold light in the center of the building ahead.

"Where's the truck with our bags?"

"Where did Karen go?"

"What is this, like Capture the Flag?"

"Is that fence electrical? Electrified? Whatever?"

"Craig?"

He heard the voices around him. Like they were coming from a mile away. He reached back into the bag.

"What is that, a heart monitor?"

"Craig?"

It was an elastic strap. A device on the opposite side of the plastic clasp. A small illustration printed on it. A stylized man putting it on at an angle over his chest.

"It's a camera, I think."

"Craig!"

He fell back on his ass when Kat shook his shoulder. His teeth clacked shut, and he dropped both the phone and the camera. Flung his arms out to keep from falling all the way to his back.

Kat kneeled down until her nose was almost touching his. "What's happening?"

Craig didn't have the heart to tell her that he had no idea.

Chapter Six

Ty stepped toward the gate. His hand up in front of him and shaking. "So, is it?"

Jeff looked up from his new phone. "Is it what?"

"Is it electrified?"

"How should I know?"

As Ty got closer, the crowd grew quiet. The expectation was like a string tugging at Craig's back. Making him lean away. He looked around for a piece of wood. Into the trees to notice everything appeared to be covered in glistening dew. Like it had just finished raining.

He grabbed a handful of his own shirt. Then released it to look at his open hand.

Ty's finger got closer. Craig hitched in a breath and threw his own arms out. "Wait!"

Ty jerked back. Looked at Craig like he was a murder clown that had just jumped out of a dark doorway. "Damn, man!" His nervous grin twitched to show his teeth like a strobe light. "Don't do that shit!"

"Use your elbow," Craig said.

"What?"

Jeff stood up with a knowing nod. "He's right. If you touch it with your hands, your fingers might tighten, like a spasm. You hang on and burn up."

Craig kept himself from sending a sarcastic thank you Jeff's way. Kept his gaze locked on Ty. "Right?"

"Yeah. Okay." Ty nodded, then turned back to the gate. Edged his elbow in front of him. "Right."

Craig felt the buzz in the air overhead as Ty covered the remaining inches. Just before Ty made contact, Craig forced his eyes open wide.

Blinding fire exploded from the metal chain link and Ty's dark skin. A pop that sounded like an exploding bicycle tire. Ty flew back like he was plunging into a pool. Hit the pavement on his back. The tight muscles keeping his chin tucked into his chest saved the back of his head from slamming into the concrete.

Selena screamed. Rushed over to press her face into Jeff's chest. Marcy fell to her knees, staring at Ty's body as it slid a few feet to fetch up against Craig's shins.

Where his arm had touched the gate, the skin had pulled apart into the shape of a pink tree. Leafless and dead like it stood alone on a winter hill. His eyes fluttered open, and he rolled over with a groan. "Definitely electrified."

Kat dropped down next to him. Helped him sit up where he cradled his burned arm in his lap. "I can't feel it. Just a tingle in my fingers."

"Good thing," Malcolm said.

Mia jumped to her full height — barely five feet of intimidation. "That was a *good* thing?"

Malcolm looked at her like she was a poisonous bug. Scooted back a step. "I mean, the fact that he can't feel it. A good thing he's not in pain. Jesus. What's your problem?"

She pointed at the old school. "Some techno bitch and her crazy bus driver dropped us off in front of Freddy Krueger's high school with nothing but a phone and an electric fence! Why don't *you* tell *me* what my problem is?"

Malcolm put both hands up. "Calm down, Yugioh."

Kelly looked up from his skateboard. "Yugioh is Japanese."

Malcolm shrugged. "So?"

Kelly pointed to Mia. "She's Chinese."

"So fucking what? Is *that* what we're gonna do now?"

Selena pushed off of Jeff's chest. "Do what? Make sure our heritage is respected?"

Malcolm's eyes bulged. "Now? You want to do this *now*?" He pointed to the trees. "Old man Logan just disappeared into the bushes like Homer Simpson."

Oz laughed into his fist. Looked around like he had been caught by surprise.

Craig held his hand up like he was requesting permission to speak. "I hate to say it, but I agree. Let's have this discussion *after* we figure out what's going on." He held up his phone. "Anybody really look at these yet?"

Jeff nodded. "Craig's right. Let's focus."

This time, Craig couldn't help it. "Thanks so much, Jeff. I'm Korean, by the way."

Marcy looked up from where she had collapsed. "Mine already logged me in. I hit the button ... the flamey KyMera thing, and I saw the, like, finish line in the school. Then I hit the other button, and I'm streaming. Just like that." She looked up at Selena. "Jenny says hi."

Selena shook her head. Stooped for her own bag. Soon after, there was a din of quiet voices as they each streamed to their audiences. Whispering like they were afraid of being overheard.

Instead of joining them, Craig swiped his screen first

right and then left. Then up. When he swiped down, the screen image slid lower to reveal a grid of squares. In each one was each of their profile pictures.

When he pressed Jeff's picture, the screen filled with the live video from Jeff's KyMera phone. His voice from the small speaker a split-second behind the one from a few feet away.

"And then she said we had to tap the plate in the auditorium. After that, the bus driver dipped. Then Ty got shocked on the fence. Guys, I think we need help."

Craig was soothed by Jeff's calm.

He swiped to the left, and Selena's feed came up. She was sobbing. Begging her followers to do something — *anything* — to get her out. Even then she looked gorgeous.

Another swipe, and Kelly's video was a static image of him sitting with Oakridge Academy in the background. Craig thought something was wrong with the feed, until he noticed the sweat rolling down his cheeks. Kelly was just frozen with fear.

He didn't bother scrolling through the rest.

He sat back on his heels.

"This is really starting to hurt," Ty said.

Craig thought he was talking to his phone. Looked over to find Ty looking back. Like he was asking him for help, only he didn't know how.

Craig scooted closer. "Can you get your shirt off?"

Ty shrugged. Winced at the movement. Then he nodded. "I think so. Why?"

Craig pointed to the burn. It was seeping clear fluid. "We should probably wrap that up. For the ... bleeding, or whatever. And probably so the pressure can, I don't know, ease the pain a little?"

"Yeah, okay."

By the time they had his shirt off, Ty was sweating.

Breathing like he had just run a mile flat out. Craig felt Kat's hand guiding his as he took the T-shirt and carefully slid it under Ty's elbow.

"Just do it, man," Ty hissed.

Kat grabbed Ty's wrist as Craig wrapped and pulled, tying a tight knot over the worst of the burn. It smelled like a charred hotdog, and Craig almost threw up when his stomach growled.

His body needed what it needed. He hadn't eaten in hours. Maybe somebody had some of those Sour Patch Kids left.

Ty took a deep breath. Lifted his arm and made a tentative fist. "Hey," he gasped. "Hey! That ain't bad. Where'd you learn to do that?"

"I did a YMCA thing a few summers ago. First aid and lifeguard stuff." Craig was too ashamed to admit he had mostly been there to watch Brad Lowell swimming laps in a Speedo. At least something useful stuck.

"Should we put these on?" Ira asked.

Craig looked over to see him holding up the strap camera. He shrugged. "Are we still going to try to get inside and win?"

"I don't know."

Malcolm aimed his thumb at his own chest. "I sure as shit am. You queers wanna dress each other, be my guest."

Jeff put his hand on Malcolm's shoulder. "Come on."

Malcolm shook it off. "No, fuck that." He pointed at his phone. Then at Jeff's face. "You been riding my audience this whole time anyway. But not today. I'm better on my own, and I'm gonna win. They want it, they got it."

Craig noticed he had the strap on his chest already. The tiny camera pointing straight ahead from below his bulging pecs.

Kat's was around her waist. Adjusting it up above her

belly button. As the rest of them followed suit, Jeff nodded. Turned to look at the path leading up to the school. "Just gonna walk right in the front door?"

Malcolm shrugged. "Maybe. If it's like every first-person shooter, why not? The way is always marked. You can't veer off it, and there's always ammo scattered all over the room before the boss."

Ira finished buckling the small clasp behind his back. "Unless it's an open-world sandbox game. Then you can go anywhere."

Malcolm's eyes widened with his grin, and he pointed at Ira's face. "Exactly! I'm out, bitches."

He turned around and brought his phone up as he stepped into the weeds at the edge of the path. "Let's go, my fellow Malcomtents. Get this side quest done."

The loud creaking of an old rotten board. A snapping branch. A rush of leaves as the snare closed over Malcolm's leg. His hip popped with a wet tearing sound as the rope jerked his foot out and up, and Malcolm screamed as he flew into the air.

Fifteen feet later, he bounced to a halt at the top of the rope's arc. His new phone flipped through the air. His wallet slipped from his pocket to tumble to the brush beneath him. His arms waved as he swung back and forth, dangling from a branch upside down.

Marcy shook her head. Clutched at Selena, and they both fell into a desperate embrace.

Kat took a step. Paused before looking back at Craig. "That's so dangerous. He could have broken his neck."

Craig nodded. "He might be okay."

A *whoosh* of flames punctuated his statement, and a burning arrow arced out of the trees. It hit Malcolm in the side, sounding like a baseball slamming into the center of a catcher's mitt.

Craig couldn't be sure one of the screams that rose up around him wasn't his.

Malcolm thrashed as flames covered him from waist to toes, his scream hoarse and desperate. Like a train whistle in the night.

Craig pressed into the group. They clung to each other as Malcolm burned. Another two arrows flew from the trees.

One skipped off Ira's shoulder. He jerked out of Craig's arms with a yelp of surprised pain, the fire following him down to the ground. Craig threw himself down with him. Spread out to cover the flame.

Wind from their landing blew it out, but the arrow that slammed into Mia's chest splattered fire into her face and hair.

She erupted into a screaming ball of flames, and they all threw themselves away from her.

Craig rolled away from Ira. Stretched his hands toward Mia, but Kat was there. In his arms holding him back as Mia ran a handful of steps before crashing down and burning. Black smoke rolled from a blaze that feasted on her small body.

Kat buried her face in his neck. Gasped sobs into his ear. Craig tore his gaze from where Mia fell to look up at Malcolm. Now completely still as the flames consumed him. Eyes closed and face turning black. The rope burned in two, and Malcolm dropped to the ground. Fire splashed like water, sizzling into the bushes to die in wisps of smoke.

What had seemed like dew must have been something to keep the fire from spreading. Somebody had planned this very thing.

"This was on purpose," he breathed.

Kat straightened up to look around. "What was?"

Craig noticed they were alone in front of the gate. Smoke blew across his face, burning his eyes.

He looked toward the building to see the rest of them in a ragged line, running toward the front door. Ira broke away and turned around. "Come the fuck *on*!"

Craig squinted through the smoke. Up at the trees. Watching for more arrows as he pulled Kat to her feet. He felt the phone in his hand. Stuffed it into his pocket. Pulled her along to stumble behind him.

"What are we going to do?" she asked.

He could barely make sense of what was happening, let alone know what they might do next. What kind of sick game was this? Was this part of the game or had someone infiltrated it to hunt them down? Nothing made sense.

"Craig?"

He looked up at Kat.

"Run."

Chapter Seven

Craig held Kat at his side as they jumped into a run. Ira hung back from the group ahead. Selena and Marcy cowering in Jeff's shadow as he guided them to the wall next to the broken steps.

Ira looked back at Craig, then to either side like he had lost his sense of direction. A curl of smoke rose from his shoulder where the arrow had bounced off.

Just before Craig and Kat got to him, Ira darted off the path toward a row of thick bushes. Slipped in a churn of mud. Slid the rest of the way into the cover of dark leaves.

Craig pulled Kat away from where Jeff stood with his back to the decaying stone. Through the swampy lawn where his shoes sank in the clumping mud next to where Ira had entered the bushes.

Kat fell against him. Craig went to his knees. They dug through to get their backs to the weeds looking out through the bushes. Jeff and the girls still standing there. Oz and Kelly nowhere to be seen.

A hand was suddenly on Craig's shoulder.

He screamed before he realized it was Ira. He clamped his teeth shut and slapped a dirty hand over his mouth.

"Sorry, sorry," Ira breathed.

"She burned up," Kat whispered. "They're ... they're dead. What the fuck is going on here?"

Black smoke continued to roll from the charred bodies. Craig could still smell the sickly-sweet aroma of cooking meat.

Ira dropped back to sit on his heels. Stared at Oakridge Academy with his mouth agape.

When Craig had first gotten his driver's license, he'd been particularly careful when driving in the rain. Feeling the car skip on the water always tightened his guts. Nausea swelled up into his chest. Taste of copper on his tongue.

His mother had told him it was better to learn to drive in the rain than to avoid it, because if he ever got in a situation where he needed to — he wouldn't be able to.

So he forced himself. Pushing his ability and his confidence until it was okay. Until driving in the rain was normal. Until his instincts, and responses to wet conditions, were perfectly honed.

One night, coming home from Kat's after doing a video at the outlet malls, he drove through a storm on I-70. It was no problem for *him*, but the motorcycle ahead of him on the exit wasn't as lucky. A man with a woman hanging on behind him.

He had asked himself why somebody would be out in this kind of weather on a bike. Had they gotten caught in a surprise storm? Were they that hardcore?

At the top of the hill, the bike slid off the road and disappeared over the edge. The woman was in the air, tumbling like a falling star. Only a split second that seemed to spill into an infinity.

Craig fought his instinct to slam on the brakes. Coasted

to a stop past where the bike had gone off the road. He called 911, surprised by his calm. Told the dispatcher what he had seen.

"Is the driver or the passenger injured?"

Craig couldn't see from where he was. He shook his head, but remained silent.

"Ma'am, are they still alive?"

He looked at the phone with a sneer. *Ma'am?* Dropped the phone on the seat and jumped out into the rain.

He ran to the shoulder, sliding on the wet gravel. Over the edge, guided by the motorcycle's running lights. The putter of its dying engine.

He got to the bottom by sliding down on his ass. Hands and feet out like a water strider gliding along the surface of their pool when he forgot to put shock in it. The bike was in a few inches of water. Smoke coughed up into his face. He felt around for the driver. Slapping at the water like he would find them by watching the waves. He froze when he saw them.

The man sat with his legs out in front of him. One arm cradled in his lap.

Craig splashed toward him. "Hey! Are you okay?"

He made a wide circle to get in front of him, then stopped when he saw the woman in a broken heap of denim. Just her back. Hair in a wet tumble around her head.

Craig looked away. Back to the man who sat staring at the woman's body. Mouth slack. Eyes wide. Not actually seeing. "She's dead." He looked up to meet Craig's gaze. "I killed her."

Craig had avoided driving in the rain ever since. Too many dreams about drowning in puddles.

Ira's face looked just like the man's had that night.

Empty of everything but shock. For a moment, Craig could hear the sound of rain on open water.

Kat's fingers dug into his arm. "She's dead."

He heard the man's voice again. *I killed her*.

Craig took her hands in his. Guided them to her lap. "I know, sweetie. But *we're* not dead."

"Why?"

"Because we're in the bushes."

Her lips curled into a growl. "No, Craig. Why is she dead?"

Craig took his hands back. "I don't know."

"Who did it?"

"I don't *know*."

She covered her face with both hands. "She was little. Not a threat to anyone. Who would target her, or *any* of us?"

Craig turned away. Avoided looking at the dark smoking lumps. Felt the phone digging into his hip. He pulled it out of his pocket. Brought it back to throw it away from him.

Then he pulled it back in. Swiped it open.

"This is a phone, right?"

Ira shrugged. "I guess."

"Then shouldn't it make calls?"

"Maybe."

Craig swiped in every direction. Tapped everywhere on the screen. No matter what, it was always the same pair of icons, and the screen of profiles.

Malcolm and Mia's pictures were grayed out.

Craig clicked on the KyMera icon. The overhead view of the grounds. Little red dots. One green one. The gold prize blinking in the auditorium.

He swiped away. Lowered the phone to his thigh. Dropped his chin to his chest. Looked at the tiny camera peeking out from the folds of his shirt. Straightened up with the phone in front of him.

He brought the profiles back up. Clicked on his own. The image split into two videos. The feed from his body cam. It saw the bottom of his phone. Trembling leaves. Mia's smoke drifting into the courtyard.

The upper half of the video was from the camera in his phone. His pale face. Staring in shocked confusion.

Comments scrolled by.

P_KIDDY — how did you do the flaming arrows?

Samantha sam — faaaaaaaaaaaaaaaaake

Artemis99 — SO COOL

Carmenita   yay best collab ever!

JamJam Gaming — Of course it's fake. It's called a STUNT for a reason.

B Giles — NOOOOOOO Malcolm died so quick

HE CLICKED OVER TO SELENA. Her face up close in the camera, distorted by being so close. A fish-eyed view of a beauty vlogger. "Please, please, please," repeated on a loop as she tried to look in every direction at once. Her body cam showed only Jeff's back. She begged viewers to call the police, hell, even the Army. Told them where they were.

"Someone's gonna come, right? I mean, they have to?" Kat said.

"I hope," Craig said.

"What if they all think it's staged, fake?" Ira asked. "And nobody calls anyone?"

Craig clicked over to Ty. Nothing from his phone camera. Maybe it was in his pocket. Or broken from the shock? The body cam was working, though. A close-up of the front wall of Oakridge Academy as he crept up close to Jeff, Marcy, and Selena.

JOHNAKAJACK — those shoes were fresh tho
   dante819 — tap that phone big g
   Benji Sing — WINNERRRRRRRRRRRRR

IRA'S BODY cam was an image of Craig hunkered down in the weeds in front of him. The same as Kat — whenever she lowered her hands to give whoever was watching a better view.

Craig lowered his phone again. "That's the question, really."

Kat pawed at his shoulder. "What is?"

Craig took her hand. Gave it a reassuring squeeze before letting it go. "We know our followers are watching. But the question is — who *else* is watching?"

Chapter Eight

Ray Wardell pulled himself through the hole in the floor, upset with himself for how hard he was breathing from a short run and a climb up a ladder.

He drew his knees up and stood with a grunt. Wilkie Ryder stood at the slim window. A mountain of hair and muscle, he turned to nod before lowering his bow to lean it against the wall.

Ray eased into a camp chair in the corner. Winced at his burning knees. Pointed at the window with one hand and grabbed his thermos with the other. "That was a hell of a shot."

Wilkie smiled with only half his mouth. Growled his amusement.

Ray poured a cup of steaming coffee. Caught the smell of bourbon underneath it. Grinned his appreciation as he lifted the plastic cup in a toast. "That kid was bigger than his britches for sure. I had to use the power of prayer to keep from slapping the ever-living shit right out of him."

Wilkie pulled his ghillie suit from a hook. A mass of leaves and moss netting that looked just like the terrain down on the ground. It even had the glisten of the fire retardant they had sprayed on everything this morning.

Ray took a sip. "That second shot, though."

Wilkie froze.

Ray blew steam from the surface of the coffee. "I figured you were going for the little one, but she was in the crowd."

Wilkie nodded.

"You got her with the third one."

Wilkie shrugged as he stepped into the suit. Got it to his waist before looking up. "Sorry."

A harsh whisper. Ray was satisfied with the emotion in it. The genuine sorrow he heard. He tipped his cup to him again. "You got her, though. And they screamed and scattered and realized just how unimportant they really are."

Wilkie wore his half-smile again as he raised the suit to his shoulders. Pushed his arms through.

Ray pulled his phone out. A KyMera job just like the ones Mrs. Beal had given the children. Only his was unlocked.

Instead of opening the screen, he laid it face-down on his thigh. Took another long sip. The pain in his abdomen spiked. Burning pressure that subsided after he held his breath.

He caught the worry in Wilkie's eye. Waved it away. "It ain't nothing. Just a spot of bother here on my last ride. I gotta couple weeks as near normal as I can be. Then the treatments start. Then I'll be nothing. That is, if I even make it."

Wilkie looked away as he raised the hood of the ghillie suit. He never liked it when Ray talked about his cancer. About what it was going to do to him. Ray knew he was worried about him. But he was also worried about *himself*.

Without Ray, he'd be back in the ward, dribbling

through the drugs and getting electroshock treatments. Without Ray, he'd just be a ghost.

But soon, Ray would be a ghost.

Ray pointed at the window again. "This place ... this place where I was taught how to be a man ... how to maintain the masculine ideal. It was sacred. It turned out so many great men, brought low by the matriarchal shift in a society that values feelings over all else. Results? Victory? Success? They don't matter if one single unique flower ends up with a damaged petal."

Ray buried his disgust under a gulp of scalding liquid.

"And these kids, and everybody watching them, are getting a taste of what this shift is gonna cost us. America is fucked, my friend. Unless we can bring masculine excellence back to the forefront of what *fathers* are supposed to teach *sons*."

He poured another cup while shaking his head. "And the *girls*. Getting views with their skin. Getting *power*. Then using that power to protect the very thing they sold for pennies to *get* that power. Shame a woman for being fat, and the barn burns. Shame a man for being fat, and it's a chuckle. And don't get me started on the rest."

He settled deeper into his chair. "Be a man. Be a woman. What else is there? And if you're going to be a man, be the *best* one. Simple shit here. Learned the hard way. The way you're *supposed* to learn things. This generation is soft. They need to get this right. Instead of screaming and scattering, they should be uniting. And not just them out there in the courtyard. *All* of them. A youth united is a generation of workers. Of producers. Of *value*!"

He looked down at some of the coffee that had spilled out onto his thumb. A small lick to clean it off. "I would have respected that dumb blond kid if he had taken a swing at me. If he had backed up his bullshit, I would have shaken his hand. But like all of 'em these days, he never learned the right lesson."

He sighed as he pulled the phone up. "Go teach them that lesson, son."

Wilkie was a silent shadow that slipped out of the blind like dust scattering in the breeze.

Ray opened the screen. Smiled at the two gray pictures. Scrolled through the ten remaining profiles. "Children should be seen and not heard."

He tapped on the first one. Selena Sanchez. Nothing interesting. Only the whining he expected. Next to her friend, Marcy. A little hanger-on. Following in Selena's path because she didn't have one of her own.

Jeff's silence made him pause. No commentary. No speaking into the camera. Just the view of his body cam swinging back and forth as he surveyed his situation.

Like a man.

Ray decided to watch that one as he moved down the line. Dismissing one after another. Until he came to Craig. An unlikely person to gain his attention. Then his respect. Using the camera not to cry about the situation, but rather to implore the empty minds of his followers for help.

"This isn't a stunt or a collab." Calm and steady with no hysterics or drama. "It's all real. People are dying here. We need you to send help."

Ray didn't bother reading the comments. He could barely decipher any of the nonsense scrolling by. Instead, he watched Craig's face. Another one he would have to watch.

He may not have *looked* like a man, but he was sure as hell acting like one.

Chapter Nine

Craig watched the comments. Not the words, but the tone.

They all thought it was staged.

He clenched his jaw as he sat back in disbelief. Realized he would only make their belief deepen if he begged. Crying into the camera like the dramatic queen many of them thought he was.

But he didn't feel good about putting the phone back in his pocket. The number of people watching. Commenting in real time. He'd never had views like that before.

He stayed crouched down as he turned into the weeds. Pushed through a few feet deeper into the bushes. He felt the electric buzzing in the air as Kat grabbed at his shirt tail. Saw the criss-cross pattern of the chain-link in front of him.

The smell of Ty's burn flooded his memory.

He stopped so fast, Kat ran into him, almost driving him into the fence.

He pushed back against her. "Go back!"

"Why?"

He pulled a branch aside. "It's the fence. It must go all around us."

She scrambled back like she'd witnessed a snake rising up from its coils. He almost looked down at his phone to see how the viewers had taken it.

Kat continued her frantic crab-walk until she was out of the bushes, sitting exposed in the growing shadow of the Oakridge Academy building. She froze with the realization of where she was. Looked to either side in a panic. Craig decided to end her indecision.

He grabbed Ira's arm as he rushed from cover. Dragged him into motion before reaching down to pull Kat to her feet, and they were running. To the corner of the building. Along the wall to join the crowd standing glued to the ground right next to the rotting entrance.

Craig ignored Selena and Marcy. They were chirping into their cameras at a mile a minute. Almost oblivious to the danger they were reporting to their followers.

He grabbed Jeff's wrist, but Jeff pulled his hand away with a disgusted sneer.

Craig would have to worry about Jeff's homophobia later. "It looks like the fence goes all the way around."

"How do you know?"

"I was on the crew that built it."

"What?"

Craig couldn't help smiling at Jeff's blank confusion. He pointed into the bushes he'd just emerged from. "I saw it. Some at least from the front gate over there to what … twenty yards? I think it's safe to assume it goes the whole way."

Jeff nodded. "Okay. Yeah."

Ira pulled at Craig's shoulder. "I don't think it's Capture the Flag."

Kat slapped at Selena's hands. "We should get rid of the phones."

Selena drew back with a snarl. "What's your problem, bitch?"

"And the cameras, too!" Kat reached for the band hugging her waist.

Marcy jumped forward and grabbed Kat's wrist. "You can't do that!"

Kat slapped her hand away. Pulled her camera free and dropped it on the ground. "But that's how they're tracking us."

Selena rolled her eyes. "Of course it is." She turned to Marcy. "Why do you care what *she* does? Let her drop her phone and lose her chance to win." She looked back at Kat with a satisfied smile. "They're *obviously* tracking us, but we need the phones if we expect to follow the map to our prize."

Ty pushed off the wall. "It's in the middle of the building. In the auditorium. You need a map to get to the center of a *building*?"

Selena rolled her eyes. "Whatever. You still need the phone to win. How can you tap if you don't have the phone Karen gave us?"

Ty shrugged. Winced before holding his arm against his chest. "Maybe we don't need to worry about tapping at all."

Selena smirked into her camera. "A million dollars?"

Ira pointed to where Mia lay smoldering. "What about that?"

Selena shrugged.

Kat stared at the phone. Held it up so the camera could get a good view of her face, but she didn't say anything.

"I'm telling you," Ira said. "It's *not* Capture the Flag."

Jeff looked out over their heads. Then he focused on Craig. "So, what do we do?"

Craig wanted to shout in his face — *How the hell do I know?* Instead, he put himself in the center of the group with a sigh. "We need to come up with a strategy, but I don't think any of us are qualified."

Jeff narrowed his eyes. "What's *that* mean?"

Kat cowered against the wall with the phone against her chest. "Shouldn't we get out of the open?"

Craig swept his arm over the group. "We have a quarterback, a couple gamers, and three beauty vloggers."

Ty lifted his good arm, palm up. "Come on, man."

"*Lifestyle* vloggers and one *life guide*," Craig shouted. Then he ducked his head and lowered his voice. "Whatever, Ty. Does it really matter what I call you? The point still stands."

Ty pointed to his phone. "It might matter to *them*." He looked at the screen, and his eyes widened in surprise. "Look how many are watching. Thank you, guys. I couldn't do what I do without your support."

Craig could barely believe Ty was actually thanking his viewers for watching him get electrocuted. But it was the engagement they had all trained themselves to seek. The response. The attention.

He looked up to catch Jeff's gaze. Intent and knowing.

He noticed Jeff's phone was in his pocket.

"Dude," Ty said. "They loved it when I touched the gate. I got ten thousand subscribers. Ooh, and look at this. My boy, Johnny just donated to the channel. Thanks for the bits, J!"

Craig held Jeff's gaze as he nodded. Slid his own phone into his pocket.

"Maybe we can convince our audience that this is real if we work together," Kat said.

The others just stared at her.

Her face collapsed into tears. "We don't really want to compete against each other right?"

Their silence was devastating confirmation.

She looked from face to face. Finally settling on Craig as she whispered, "Right?"

Craig looked away to find Jeff still staring, feeling a shift in how Jeff regarded him. No longer like a victim. Certainly not like a peer. Craig felt a chill when he realized what it was he saw in Jeff's face. The golden boy quarterback now saw the tiny Korean queer as an adversary.

Craig pulled Kat away from the wall. "I think that's the point."

Ira looked back and forth between Craig and Jeff. "What do you mean? What point?"

Jeff nodded like he'd decided something. "No ... it's not Capture the Flag."

Craig made sure Kat was behind him at the edge of the group. "It's Battle Royale."

He could tell they all knew what that meant.

It was a contest. One or two winners in a group of twelve. Only two of them were already dead. The odds of winning had improved.

But according to the smoking corpses, so was the chance of dying.

There would be no working together. Craig knew that when it came down to it, this game would be every person for themselves.

Chapter Ten

Wilkie cased along the edge of the wooden garden shed on the east side of the courtyard. Even if he'd been walking in his birthday suit instead of his ghillie suit, the kids were too busy arguing among themselves to see him.

Too busy talking into their phones.

It left them with an inability to focus. To plan and act. They could only *react*.

Wilkie slid into the opening of the crooked sliding door. Back to the rear corner where he could crouch in the deep shadows and watch.

It was like any hunting. Watch the prey. Learn their habits. Their weaknesses. Use their ignorance against them.

Two of the kids broke off from the rest. One with long hair covered by a beanie that made him look like he was sporting a sweeping mullet. The other juggled a skateboard and an inhaler. Took a big pull from the plastic nozzle before stowing it in his pocket and pulling out his KyMera phone.

Wilkie was reminded of his own phone. Cursed himself

for keeping it in the pouch on his waist. It was hard for him to remember to use it. That there were people on the other side almost begging to watch what was happening.

He didn't know how it worked — or why it was important — but Ray had told him to use the camera as much as he could. Simple enough.

Ray told him to do it, so he did. And he was gentle with his corrections. Not yelling. Just showing disappointment whenever Wilkie fucked up.

That hurt way worse than if he'd just kicked his ass.

Like when he missed his shot on the little Jap girl. He'd almost wanted to cry. But having tears on his cheeks when Ray had climbed inside would have been embarrassing.

Masculine excellence begins in the heart.

Wilkie turned the phone so it had a good view of the shed's interior as he set it on a dusty shelf over his shoulder. A tiny adjustment, then he crouched back down. Reached into his pouch.

It was like duck hunting. Decoys and calls.

The kid with the long hair — Wilkie decided to call him Mullet. That kid did an impressive jump over a pile of overgrown debris that Wilkie knew had once been a brick and iron barbecue smoker.

A kicking twist with athletic flair. A tinge of jealousy. Wilkie could pick up houses, but he looked like an uncoordinated ox while doing it. Just once, he'd like to know what it was like to feel graceful.

Maybe smaller. Taking up less space. Moving like a dancer.

He heard the music that would play as he drifted through a room like water. Flowing with easy movement. Something soft. Light guitars. Maybe a saxophone.

Mullet hurdled another obstacle, crouching down and

turning back to look at the building, not realizing he was leaving his back completely exposed to view from the tree line. Or the shed.

Wheezy came over to sit next to him, moving with far less skill than Mullet. Dropping down to gasp at his side. Both of them chattering into their phones in carrying whispers.

"Did you guys fucking see that shit? I wish I had my drone."

"I think I'm gonna die. All that smoke and the running."

"So ditch the board."

"I can't. I'm gonna sign it after we win. The top comment gets it ... or the top comment that's in the United States, anyway."

Wilkie shook his head as he pulled the tape player up. The Sony Walkman TCM-323. A standard cassette recorder with a built-in speaker.

He'd found it at a vintage audio swap meet. In a pile of other colorful bricks. It was the only one that didn't have corrosion on all the battery terminals.

Old batteries burst inside. Leaked acid all over. Sometimes down into the electronics. Wilkie took them and rebuilt them. New belts. New capacitors. Cutting and polishing the plastic. Recreating the logos and lettering by hand.

A unit without corrosion was a better start.

Just like how he made duck decoys while back in the hospital. Bent over the bench for hours, staring through a magnifying glass as he put highlights in the ducks' eyes.

Soldering new leads to a board.

He put the Walkman on the floor. Pressed play. Turned the volume up before stepping back. Tilted his head to admire how the black plastic gleamed in the light bleeding through the shed doors.

He also used to make duck calls. Before guys from the TV made them so popular. Painstakingly detailed as the decoys. A good call could mean the difference between a successful hunt and going home empty-handed.

He nodded at the cassette recorder. It was a good call.

The sound of a ringing phone came from the little speaker. As clear as it would have been on the day it was manufactured.

"What's that?"

Wilkie smiled when the call worked immediately.

Mullet turned to stare at the shed as the ringing continued.

Wilkie knew the sound would bring them in just like the ducks. First a question. Then a return call. Then wheeling around to explore the familiar sound. Then dropping from the sky to get comfortable in the water.

Mullet came at a crouch. Wheezy close behind him. Wilkie tensed in preparation.

Instead of stepping in carefully, Mullet stood to his full height before pushing the sliding doors apart. Walked in like he owned the shed and everything in it. Wheezy pressed up against his back. Leaned out to look at the Walkman with comic confusion making his mouth fall open.

Wilkie smiled, but he didn't laugh.

Mullet turned his phone to point the camera at the floor. "What the fuck is that?"

Perfect.

Wilkie stood up and stepped in to straddle the Walkman.

Mullet and Wheezy jerked back. Looking up to where

Wilkie's head brushed the dusty rafters. Wheezy's scream brought another smile as he fell back away from Mullet.

He lost his balance and fell back on his ass, crashing his head into the edge of the door.

Wilkie reached out. Moving slowly to play it up for the camera. He felt his smile spread into a grin, and he finally laughed.

But the kid surprised him again.

Mullet dropped his phone and ducked under Wilkie's hand. Pushed outside his guard to shoot in for a takedown. He'd obviously had some training, but Wilkie estimated he had the kid by well over a hundred pounds. To Mullet, it must have felt like trying to move a bull.

Wilkie winced as Mullet's voice pierced his ear. "It's 2 V 1! It's 2 V 1!"

Wheezy was staring up like a shot deer. Eyes entirely void of understanding.

Mullet's arms snaked round Wilkie's neck for a chokehold with more strength than he would have given him credit for. His legs weren't quite long enough to make the hook at the front of his waist.

Wilkie's laugh became a cackle of glee. He took a hop, barely impeded by the weight on his shoulders. Just a few inches in the air to get his feet clear. Then he drew his legs up and threw his arms wide.

He landed flat on his back with Mullet beneath him. Cracked concrete floor, and three hundred and fifteen pounds on top of him.

"Whah!" Followed by coughing and gagging.

Wilkie rolled away, and by the time he was back on his feet, he was laughing hysterically. He drove the toe of his boot into Mullet's crotch. The kid's body scooted a few feet from the follow-through, and his next breath brought a scream of pain.

Wilkie felt the tears rolling down his face. Had to pause to catch his breath before another gale of laughter doubled him over.

Mullet's eyes bulged. Both hands covering his balls. Wilkie punched his own thigh. Over and over until the cramping pain finally made him stop laughing. He straightened with a calming sigh, then raised his boot up and stomped on Mullet's neck.

Bones broke with the sound of a horse whip cracking against flesh. Blood jetted out of the kid's mouth. Splashed down into his open eyes. His clawed hands crawled up his body as he fought for air.

Wilkie turned to the door. Wheezy had managed to stand. Held his skateboard in front of him. Stared at Mullet in dazed horror. Then lifted his gaze to the monster standing in front of him.

He whispered, "1 V 1," then took a deep breath, screaming as he launched himself in for an attack. "SUPER SAIYAN!"

Wilkie stopped the kid dead with a blow to his chest. The board flew from his hand and sent the kid to his knees, hugging himself as he choked for air. Wilkie grabbed him with one hand around his throat. Pulled him to his feet and lifted him up, choking the kid as his feet left the floor.

Wheezy's eyes bulged, and his feet kicked the air in panic. Wilkie pulled him back, then drove him down to the ground.

The air he'd struggled so hard to get left his body in a groaning *whuff*.

Eyes clenched shut, he reached into his pocket. Brought the inhaler up to his gritted teeth. Just as he triggered it, Wilkie stomped it down. Felt the kid's jaw unhinge to receive the girth of his boot heel. Saw the blood shoot up to soak his pant leg.

Wilkie pulled his foot away. Bent to grab the Walkman. Stopped the tape as he grabbed the phone from the shelf.

He aimed the camera at Mullet's blackening face. Blood surrounding it like he had lain down with an inkblot test as a pillow.

Over to Wheezy. Focusing on the torn hamburger meat of his mouth. Saw the shining white plastic of his inhaler in the growing pool of chunky blood in the back of his throat. Tiny bubbles from his last breath formed around the edges. Burst with tiny pops. Like Rice Krispies.

He put the phone and the Walkman back in the pouch on his belt.

Left the shed to move back into the cover of the overgrown trees behind it.

Another successful hunt.

Chapter Eleven

Kat moved to the corner. With her back to the group, she began pleading to the viewers. "You know me. I wouldn't lie about this. Come on, guys. *Please*."

Marcy pulled on Selena's sleeve. "Maybe she's right."

Selena pursed her lips. "It's a waste of time." She looked into the camera. "No offense, but you'll believe anything."

"Maybe a public safe word?"

Ira nodded. "Yeah. Mine's *Oklahoma*."

"Would that really work?" Marcy asked. "Somebody would use it too much, and nobody would believe it anyway."

Jeff lifted his head. "Is that a phone?"

Craig concentrated. Thought he heard it. Then wasn't sure.

"Still," Selena said. "It might be beneficial."

Craig pulled his focus back to the discussion. "In what context? This isn't an S&M dungeon." He pointed up to the trees. "Do you think the guy who fired the flaming arrows is gonna just stop because Ira yells *Oklahoma*?"

Marcy put her hand on her hip. "How do you know it's a guy? Women can't shoot arrows?"

Craig blinked like he was trying to get sand out of his eyes. He couldn't believe where the conversation was going. "Are you fucking kidding me right now?"

Kat spun around. "I see your comments. I *see* them. I'm not kidding. I'm a terrible actor. *Please!* We need help."

Ty cut his hand through the air. "This shit ain't working!"

Craig drew away from Ty's hands and pointed to Selena. "Tell her, then."

Ty shook his head. "Oz and Kelly are dead."

Kat jumped forward. "What?" She looked back to her phone. Began frantically scrolling.

Craig brought up the profile page. Oz and Kelly were grayed out. "It doesn't mean they're dead."

Ty fell back against the wall. "Go down. There's more."

Craig swiped his thumb up, and another two profiles appeared that had been hidden beneath the bottom of the screen. Both were just a square tile with a capital letter in the center. R and W.

Craig tapped the R. The screen filled with the closeup of a steaming cup of coffee sitting on the edge of the window overlooking the courtyard. In the distance was his small group huddled at the base of the wall.

Craig turned around to look up into the trees, using his phone image to guide him. "He can see us?"

"Oh, man," Ty said. "They say that Kelly swallowed his inhaler."

Craig backed up to the wall. "What does that mean?"

Kat screamed. Dropped her phone and covered her face in her hands.

He returned to the extra profiles. Tapped the W.

Small bubbles popped in the blood pooling in Kelly's shattered mouth. Then the image turned dark as the camera went into a pocket. Just the muffled audio of somebody's movement.

Kat bent over and puked on her phone. Covering the screen in a greasy puddle of barely digested candy. Swirling smears of color like a tie-dyed T-shirt.

"We're up to over five hundred thousand views," Ty said.

Craig swallowed the bile rising into his throat. Looked away from Kat's misery. Back to his phone. He swiped back to the R profile. Tapped it, but the image was dark. As if he'd turned off the phone. Him.

R.

"Ray," he said.

Ty snorted. "The bus driver?"

"Why not? Malcolm was giving him shit. Maybe it ... I don't know. Like, drove him insane with anger."

Jeff looked at him with his eyes narrowing in thought. Craig wished he would say something. Then maybe he could tell what he was thinking. It might tell him what he was planning.

"Fuck y'all," Ty said. "I mean, no offense, but if it's Battle Royale, then it's every man for himself."

Marcy took an unsteady step forward. "Or *woman*."

Ty rolled his eyes. "Jesus, whatever. All I'm saying is I'm out."

Without another word, he pushed off the wall. Jogged around the steps past the front door and moved into the thick grass to run under the windows in a crouch.

"He's right," Selena said.

Kat was still bent over. Hands on her knees. A string of spit stretching down to dangle over the space between her feet.

Marcy shook her head like she was trying to shake cobwebs from her hair. "What do you mean? Splitting up? Then I'd be —"

"You and me," Selena said. "*Just* you and me. Like what got us here in the first place."

Marcy grinned as she sighed in relief. Looked at Selena with naked worship.

Craig stilled the disgust threatening to fill his face. Kept his mouth shut as Marcy and Selena pulled each other in and moved around Kat to disappear around the corner.

Kat pushed herself up. Wiped her mouth on her forearm. Reached for Craig. He moved around Ira to take her hand. Pulled her against him and moved to Ira's other side. He and his two best friends facing Jeff.

Ira broke the awkward silence. "There are three rules that will dramatically improve our odds."

Jeff crossed his arms. "In a Battle Royale?"

Ira nodded. "I think so."

"Even knowing that eventually, only one of us can win?"

Ira jumped forward to stick his finger in Jeff's chest. "But all of us can *live*."

Jeff acted like the finger wasn't there. "Then what are the rules?"

Ira yanked his finger back like Jeff's chest was a sizzling cooktop, then looked back at Craig with less certainty than was in his voice just a moment ago. "Rule one ... squad mode."

When Jeff snorted laughter, Ira raised a hand as if asking for patience. "Seriously. It's better to stick with a group as long as you possibly can. A band of trusty teammates can always best somebody without a squad."

Jeff nodded. "Okay, then what's the second rule?"

"Always keep moving."

Craig felt like he was standing in front of a freezer. A chill rolled up over his shoulders. They had been here for a long time. More than enough time for somebody to have made better plans. Or to come up behind them.

He sneaked a look over his shoulder. Released his held breath when he saw nobody was there.

"It's harder to hit a moving target," Ira continued.

Jeff spread his hands. "We are not, in fact, moving right now."

Ira nodded. Pointed to the front door. "I'm sure not gonna go that way. It screams *trap* to me."

Craig glanced back up at the trees. "And what's the third rule?"

Ira paused to look up at Jeff. Then he stepped aside to make room for him. Jeff nodded before stepping into the group and making them a squad.

Ira sighed with relief. Gave a nervous smile as he looked at each of them in turn. "We loot the fuck up."

Chapter Twelve

Craig had expected Jeff to take over, to start leading them right away. But then he realized they were all looking at *him*.

He pulled Kat behind him. Moved toward the corner that Selena and Marcy had gone around. Not because it was a good direction to head in, but because it was away from the trees where the arrows had come from.

"I knew it," Ira said.

Craig looked back, but Ira wasn't looking at him. Instead, his gaze was fixed several feet in the direction where they had been walking. Craig followed his gaze, then pulled up in dread.

Under the first window down the side of the building was an old section of wooden fencing. Leaning against the wall at an angle. Under a broken window. Like somebody had put it there as a makeshift ladder to gain entry into the building.

"You think Selena and Marcy did it?"

Kat sneered. "And risk breaking a nail?"

"No," Craig said. "I don't think it *is* an open sandbox world."

Jeff pushed past him. "It's the path. Like *Resident Evil* where it only *looks* like you have a choice, but everything is pointing you to one thing."

"Yeah," Ira agreed. "Like the yellow ladders and shit in *Village*.

Craig had never played any games from that series, but he knew what they were talking about. Streets blocked with wreckage. Doors that were always locked. It gave the illusion of choice, but you always ended up right where the developers wanted you to go. Usually into the jaws of a drooling monster.

Jeff eased to the section of fence to peek over the window ledge. "Yep."

Craig could have jumped as hard as he could and still not seen inside. "What?"

Jeff turned back to study the fence. He looked unsure of its ability to hold him up. "It's an old, like, supply closet or something. Full of stuff. You know ... loot."

Craig looked back over his shoulder. Expected to see Ray running around the corner with a gun. Like he had actually seen him, Craig jumped forward and scrambled up the fence. In spite of its appearance, the fence didn't creak or wobble.

He climbed through at the top, and before he had planted his feet, Kat was already coming through. Jeff's hands on her waist to help her up. Craig wondered why he hadn't offered the same help to him.

Ira came through with a dazed smile. "See? It was put there to guide us inside."

Craig stepped back to make room for Jeff. "Then maybe we shouldn't have done it. If it's what they want us to do."

Jeff laughed as he stood up. "Is there really a *good* way to go? Besides, if this is a game, then maybe it rewards us for making the right choices, for choosing the right path."

Craig kept quiet as he moved to see where he was. An old couch against the wall in front of the door. Cabinets and shelves. School desks pushed to one side.

"Hey look," Ira shouted in a stage whisper. "MREs!"

"What's that?" Kat asked.

Jeff opened a desk drawer. "Army food." He pulled his hand out with a triumphant smile, holding a rusty butter knife.

"Nice," Craig said. "We can fight back by raising their cholesterol."

Jeff stuck the knife in his back pocket. "What have *you* found?"

Kat pointed at a small white box covered in dust. "Is that a first-aid kit?"

Craig shook his head as he turned away from Jeff's smirk. Opened a drawer of his own. Caught his breath when he saw metal shining. He pulled out a brass lighter. Popped the lid open with a ringing *clink*. Struck the wheel, and a flame flickered from the wick.

He shrugged. "Might be better than a butter knife."

Jeff's eyebrows drew together. "How is *that* thing still working?"

Craig laughed. "What do you mean? I lit it, and *poof*. Fire."

"I mean, how long does the fluid in one of those last?"

"How should I know?"

"But this place looks like it hasn't been open for decades."

"So?"

Jeff shrugged. "Just saying. Most of this stuff was here, random stuff we can make use of, but maybe that—"

Craig threw his hands out in frustration. "Maybe what?"

The voice from the window made him jump in the gap between two desks. "He's saying somebody put that lighter there on purpose. Maybe it's important."

Craig's thigh pounded against the drawer he'd just opened. The desk leg scraped across the floor with an ear-splitting squeal.

He watched between his fingers as a girl climbed through the window. The shaggy fall of Alicia Brown's afro made him relax. He rubbed at the sore spot on his leg as he worked his way out from between the desks. Looked into her face as she stood straight. Without the big glasses and the phone covering most of her face, Alicia looked very different than she had on the bus.

Both of Kat's hands were on her belly, covering the lens of her body cam. "They put it there on purpose for whom? For what?"

Craig held his finger up. "It sure wasn't put here for Alicia Brown, and you sure as fuck aren't her."

Jeff squinted into the girl's face. Then he smiled with a shake of his head and went back to opening drawers.

The girl shook her head. "No, I'm not Alicia Brown. And you bunch of racists didn't notice the difference between one Black girl and the next."

Ira stood up straight with his shoulders back in anger. "Hey!"

She spread her hands. "That's right. Even you."

Craig slipped the lighter into his pocket. "It's not like you were making it easy to figure out. Covering up and avoiding everybody."

She shrugged. "Maybe."

Jeff sighed. "Whatever. Who cares if Karen Beal thinks all Black people look alike when there's a flaming arrow up your asshole. If you're not Alicia Brown, then who are you?"

"It doesn't matter who I am."

Jeff slammed a desk drawer shut. "The hell it doesn't!"

The girl shook her head. "There's too many people watching. Too many ears listening."

Ira leaned against Kat. "She's pretty sus."

Kat nodded. "Like she's an imposter."

The girl laughed. "You think this is still a game. Well, I'm not playing."

Something about what she said. The *way* she said it. Craig suddenly knew who she was. He snapped his fingers. "I know you!"

She chopped her hand through the air. "No you don't."

"You hacked into the school database and shut class down for two weeks last year by posting a bunch of inappropriate links to the server every day."

Her smile was shy, but it transformed her face, smoothing the bitter anger away. "It was just a spam bomb. A gay porn loader."

Craig shrugged. "I mean, some of us appreciated it."

Jeff looked at the old sofa. Reached behind it and stood up with a wooden baseball bat. "So what's her name?"

The girl's smile died as she stared at Craig. He nodded before turning his attention to Jeff. "I think she's right. Too many people watching. I'll keep her secret."

"I thought we were a squad."

The girl flapped her hand as she moved to a file cabinet. Opened the drawers from top to bottom. "I'm not here for the prize. In case you haven't figured it out, there *is* no prize." She moved to the next cabinet. "I'm here for something else. If I were you, I'd lose the cameras and phones."

"We need the phones if we're gonna win. Don't we?" Jeff asked.

She laughed. "You think they're gonna let you, let any of us, walk outta here? Fuck this 'game.'"

Jeff laid the bat on his shoulder. "What are you here for?"

The girl reached into the next drawer with a cry of triumph.

Ira moved away from Kat, and Craig noticed his phone was out. The camera was focused on the girl. "What did you find?"

She shoved something into her pocket. "None of your business."

Ira nodded. "So somebody *is* leaving stuff for you?"

"Damn right," said the girl as she marched toward the door.

"Hey!" Kat shouted.

Jeff blocked her from leaving. She turned to Kat. "What?"

They all stared at her.

Kat reached behind her and popped the clasps on the body cam belt. Let it fall to the floor. "Do you know what's really happening here?"

The girl turned back to Jeff without answering. Craig tossed his hand out in dismissal. Reached around to release his own camera. "Let her go."

To his surprise, Jeff stepped aside.

The girl struggled to get the sofa out of the way. Just enough room to open the door a sliver wide enough to squeeze through, and she was gone.

Craig pointed to the pile of plastic packets Ira had found when they first got inside. "Army food, huh?"

Chapter Thirteen

Ray remembered the coat closet in the back of the classroom, how it used to be. Back when Matheson would send him in there to sit in the dark. Usually with a sore jaw.

Ray had been a handful when he first came to Oakridge Academy. Like most of the other boys. Troublemakers. Troubled.

Matheson showed them a firm hand. Later, they said he had been cruel. Especially that little Garner James. Going public with his story. Everybody calling him a "brave" survivor when all he ever really did was put an end to the finest thing Ray had ever known.

He reached up and ran his fingers over the swollen wood trim under the rusting metal coat hooks. Even now he could feel the marks carved into it. His initials joining those that had come before him.

No light except for the slice coming under the door. Tepid water out of a corrugated pitcher.

Matheson *had* been cruel. But only so he could turn

those boys into *men*. Something that was lost on Garner James.

The Army had told Ray there was no longer a place for him. Not the kind of man he had proven to be. And not one as old as him. Like he was no longer useful. Trying to run him out the way they ran out Matheson.

Pushing him away from his life's work.

Ray accepted his discharge. Pulled Wilkie out of Hampton Clearing. Got him off the drugs they'd been pumping into him by using the same cruel discipline Matheson had shown them, and just like back in the day, Wilkie came right along.

It wasn't long before they found Garner James. Cutting hair out of the back of a church. Teeth rotting out from meth. Infected tattoos smelling like a soiled diaper. And he remembered them. Through his tears, he knew what had come for him.

Ray watched as Wilkie cut him from stem to stern. Guts falling out of the slit with every scream. And he saw the gratitude in Garner's eyes.

No man wanted to live a life in which he was denied the ability to live right. Especially if he was the one to do it to himself.

Ray dropped into a painful squat. Ran his fingers along the floor. Found the split between the boards. Hooked it out to reveal the dark opening beneath.

The children only know luxury.

He pulled his phone out. Swiped down for the flashlight. Shielded his eyes as it flared to brighten the closet. Glints from the metal down in the hole.

They have bad manners, contempt for authority. They show disrespect for the elders and love chatter above exercise.

Ray pulled out the small knife. Cracked plastic. More

dirt brown than blood red. Gold logo long since worn off. The swivel was rusty, but it still opened.

Children are now tyrants, not the servants of the households.

By the light of the phone's LED, Ray put his name in the sacred wood of Oakridge. Like he had done so long ago.

They no longer rise when elders enter the room, and they terrorize their teachers.

Socrates knew, even back then, how terrible the children were becoming. How he would have wept at seeing the children from this modern era.

Ray killed the light. Flipped the phone over to look at the video feeds from the Zoomers infecting the history of Oakridge Academy. Four dead. Four without videos at all. One filming as if he was directing a documentary. Three of them chattering away, narrating their every move and emotion to a bunch of *other* Zoomers that needed to be spoon-fed what to think and feel every second of every day.

Ray stood while shaking his head in disgust. Focused on the Black kid's stream. Lowered the audio, navigating the phone controls almost as good as one of *them*. But where they had been born to it, he'd had to take classes.

Ty's face filled the screen. His million-watt grin looking a little manic. The exterior of the school bounced around behind him as he walked along the front wall.

"Y'all are right. Why dig through the bushes and shit? I'm going back. Right through the front door. Nobody would expect that, right?"

Ray leaned back to watch. Ty was coming. About time one of them did. He had painted the doors green for a reason. Maybe he'd put too much effort into making them look aged and broken like the rest of the building.

"That's right, fam. I'm wearing my vintage Nike Air's. Gotta keep 'em outta the mud."

Ray glanced down at his own boots. Solid and capable. They kept his feet dry and protected. Washed off with a splash of water. Looked as good as when he'd bought them five years ago.

Ty paused in front of the door. "Y'all sure about this? I think I might just stay outside." That grin again. "I'm just playin.' Let's go."

The comments went by faster than Ray could read them. Snatches of words. The user names like alien codes. Little smiley faces and drawings to represent everything from fire to penises spewing water drops.

Ty pushed the right-hand door open. Stepped in like there was nothing to worry about. Ray couldn't believe how ignorant these kids were. Incapable of caution or sense.

He had heard the other ones arguing in the storeroom. The echo of stomping feet. Like a herd of elephants in the dark.

"This place is musty as fuck. Like my gram's basement. But damn." The last part had been said with appreciation. Maybe a little awe.

Ray leaned forward with interest as Ty turned the camera to look up at the vaulted ceiling and the split spiral staircase. Still beautiful after so many years of neglect and abuse.

"This is some Olympus Heights shit right here."

Ray remembered when he had first seen it. Feet frozen to the ground. He could only stare up with his open mouth. Matheson had put his family's fortune into it. The beauty was mesmerizing.

Ray had cleaned the entryway tile with more toothbrushes than he could count. And look at it now …

"Which way do I go? Oh shit, hang on. Eight hundred K? Guys, I can't thank you enough for your support. This is just amaz—"

The image tilted wildly as Ty grunted in surprise. Ray chuckled as he watched Ty trip over the wire Wilkie had strung across the foyer.

The image spiraled as the phone spun away.

"Motherfucker!"

The sound of hands and knees slapping off of the greasy floor. Ty's grunts as he made it to his phone. His face hung upside down over the camera. Dirt smeared up the side of his face. Pain wrinkling his brow. "I fell on my good arm. Now they're both bad. And my Nikes are fucked."

He grabbed the phone. Sat down and spun it around to show his now-filthy shoes. The sole on the left one with a tear along the side.

"I tripped on something hanging across the bottom of the doors. Got hung up in it, and then a nail or something ... man. Look at that."

He grunted to his feet. Took a tentative step. One shoe was quiet. The other sounded like a wet fart.

"One of the air pockets is toast."

He walked toward the stairs. The left shoe continued to rip with every step.

Ray caught a comment.

PEEGUNZ — TAKE THEM OFF

"YOU KNOW what I had to do to find these Nikes, man?"

. . .

RAMONAOANOMAR — nooooooo, the hunters will get you!

RAY CLOSED the screen so he could sit in the dark for a few more moments. Put it in his pocket. Raised the knife to the underside of his forearm. Same as he'd done the first time Matheson had put him in the dark — after three days of screaming and pounding on the door.

Sitting in his own filth.

He brought the rusty blade across the skin. Felt it bite. Heard the patter of drops hit the floor. Across the toes of his boots.

He folded the knife into his pocket. When he reached for the knob, he expected to find the door locked. Felt the old panic try to bring his shoulders up. His heart thudding, driving pressure into his neck.

The cool air of the classroom rushed over him, and he smiled in relief. He would wait back in the shadows for the kids to come to him.

He'd just keep the door open.

Chapter Fourteen

Craig was surprised by the ham in the MRE. It reminded him of the Spam his mom would make on Saturday mornings. She said it was one of his father's favorites.

The crackers were too dry to eat, but Kat perked up when the small pack of Skittles fell out in a rainbow. Craig wasn't sure how such a little thing could cheer her up with so much death around them, and the threat constantly hunting them. Maybe she was in denial. Or maybe she was trying to put on a brave face for the group. Craig would try his best to do the same.

Ira nodded at his phone screen like he was agreeing to a point. "Yeah, what *does* happen when somebody taps on the plate in the auditorium while we're in here eating this garbage?"

Jeff shrugged. "We lose."

Ira leaned forward in disbelief. "And that doesn't bother you?"

"Will there still be somebody in the trees shooting flaming arrows?"

Ira sat back to look at his phone again. Eyes twitching back and forth while he read the comments.

Craig stood up and brushed his hands on the front of his thighs. "So do we try to get to the auditorium? Or do we try to hole up in here?"

Ira wondered, "If someone else wins, they've gotta let the rest of us go, right? She didn't say anything about us all needing to die, not like a real Battle Royale."

"Well, she also didn't tell us people would be trying to kill us. Why the hell isn't anybody showing up yet?" Kat said.

"Maybe they paid off the cops or something," Ira suggested. "Maybe everybody's been paid off to pretend nothing's happening."

Kat popped a candy in her mouth as she looked around with wide eyes. "Isn't all this pretty much flammable?"

Jeff looked through the door. Drew back inside and put the bat back on his shoulder. "Including us."

Craig shrugged. "Let's just go."

Jeff nodded. Pushed the sofa out of the way like it only weighed fifteen pounds. Craig looked away like it hadn't impressed him. Worried him a little too.

Kat and Ira crowded in behind him as he stepped into the dank hallway. The light of Ira's phone screen made the old dirt look like green moss.

Trash underfoot. Overturned furniture piled against the walls. Cleared down the center like a path had been opened for them.

"See?" Ira said. "A funnel. Just like in a thousand video games."

Jeff held the bat like he was ready to swing. "This place looks like *Silent Hill* without all the fog."

Ira laughed. "They got rid of all that fog in the port.

Defeated the whole purpose. You could see the edge of the map."

Boards screwed over the doors on either side of the hallway. Cabinets and tables leaning against the wall behind them. With nowhere else to go, they walked in the path's suggested direction ... deeper into the dark building.

"That was something that changed video games," Ira said, alternating his gaze between the floor and the screen. "A lot of times, it was a technological limitation. Like the processing power of the console. Or the limits of old video cards. They had to do stuff to cover up a lot of the limitations from that era."

Craig stretched to the side to peer through a tiny split in the wood of a charred door. Purple graffiti in the shape of an upside-down pentagram in the center. There was nothing through the gap but an empty room. Dust floating in the shafts of light streaming through the dirty windows.

"It changed the way games were programmed. Or the way they were *played*. Like the *Halo* Moment."

Ira slowed as his passion for his subject distracted him. Kat gave him a gentle push, and he picked his pace back up as they neared an intersection in the hallway.

Craig glanced back in time to see Jeff roll his eyes.

"Dude, nobody gives a shit about consoles your dad played," Jeff said.

"You know, once gravity was removed, the players could suddenly jump around, making it a lot harder to shoot. A moving target," Ira said, going right on despite, or maybe because of, Jeff's irritation. He turned to give Craig a smile. "Rule number two."

Back to his phone, and his steps sped up with his words. "That's how you can tell an old-school gamer from the Gen Z gamers, because the younger players would always jump all over the place, making it really hard to hit them directly."

Jeff sighed. "Like you're old enough to remember the *Halo* Moment."

Craig held his hand up. "Can everybody just be quiet?"

He pulled his phone out. Opened the map. According to the dots, his green one was right where he expected it to be. He could see other routes to the center where the golden flame pulsed, but it was clear most of those ways had been blocked.

Looking around at the way the trash was ... arranged, he confirmed his own suspicions with a nod. They *were* being funneled. He turned back to Jeff. "We really have no choice but to go wherever it leads. Unless we want to go back outside and find another way past the fence. Maybe find the power source and cut it off?"

Jeff shook his head. "I don't know what traps might be out there. And I can't imagine they leave the power source unprotected."

Kat hugged herself. "We don't know what traps are in here, either."

A choked shout from behind him made Craig spin around and drop to his knees.

Ira had made it into the intersection. Sinking through the floor.

Jeff was a wind as he sprinted by, his feet barely making any noise as he ran toward Ira.

Craig suddenly understood what he was looking at. Jumped up to chase after Jeff with Kat gasping in shock as she leapt to follow.

The old carpet in the hall had hidden the hole. Ira stepped into the middle of it.

Just before Jeff got there, Ira dropped up to his chest. His phone flew from his grip. Jeff hit his knees with his hands reaching for the edge of the carpet sliding away from him. Craig could tell he wasn't going to reach, and he still dove, lying out flat and knocking his wind out.

The tattered end of the carpet slipped through his fingers as Ira zipped through the hole and loudly crashed to the floor below.

Jeff lunged at the last second — he and Craig ended up with their heads touching at the edge of the hole, looking down into a rising cloud of dust. Craig expected Ira to be impaled on a pitchfork. Sharpened stakes. Blood pouring from a hundred puncture wounds.

Instead, Ira sat in the center of a crumpled pile of carpet. Pushed with a groan and got to his knees.

Craig rolled over with a sigh of relief.

Kat dropped with one hand on the floor and the other on Craig's chest, pushing his air out again. "Is he dead?"

Jeff rose up to sit back on his heels. "No, he's okay. For now."

Kat shouted down in a whisper, "Are you okay?"

Craig got out from under Kat's weight to look back into the hole. Ira nodded. "I think so, yeah. But I'm stuck. My foot's all wrapped up in something. I don't think I can get out on my own."

Craig reached down into the room. "I'm coming."

Ira pointed at the ceiling. "What, through the hole?"

Jeff leaned in. "No. We'll find a way down, though."

Kat stood up and stepped back from the edge. "How? The only way we can go is wherever they lead us. We need to get out of here. Someone must've heard!"

Ira fell over and rolled out of sight. "Hey! I'm up. But the door's locked or jammed or something."

"What kind of room is it?" Jeff asked.

"I don't know. Just a room. Kinda small. Me and all that wet carpet and a bunch of crap in the corners."

"Okay." Jeff nodded. "Maybe you can just sit in there and hide while we find a way to come and get you."

"Will you really?"

Jeff blinked in confusion. "Will I what?"

Ira looked away. "Come and get me?"

Craig reached again. Tears stung his eyes as he spread his fingers apart. "Of course we will. Don't *ever* think we won't."

Ira looked away like he didn't believe it.

Jeff stood up and backed away. He looked at Craig like he didn't believe it either. "Come on."

Kat nodded. She stood and took a step back into the hallway, eager to get away, making it feel like betrayal.

Craig sat back and wiped the tears away. Sniffed and cleared his throat.

"Craig?" Ira's voice sounded small and far away.

Craig leaned forward to look down into the dark room again. "Yeah."

"When you said it, I wish I would have said it back. When you told me you loved me, I should have …"

"No." Craig shook his head and jumped to his feet. "You'll still be able to say it when we come get you."

Ira nodded. Looked down at his hands. "Okay."

"Craig!" Kat hissed. "Let's go. We can save him, but we have to go!"

He remembered her crying into the phone for help. Begging for somebody to come and get them *all* out. Now so ready to leave Ira behind.

But so was he.

Craig didn't look back after he stood to follow her.

Chapter Fifteen

Wilkie watched from under the cover of the grand staircase. The hollow under the steps behind the torn wainscoting.

A bubbling fart and a sliding squeak of sound effects as somebody walked past his hiding spot. That grinning idiot that always talked about shoes.

Wilkie pulled out his knife. The Garrison TL09 he took off the redneck hunter from the truck stop out on the interstate. A kid who thought he was hot shit. Jacked-up truck. Compound bow with more pull than his shoulders could handle. A smug smirk reinforced only by youth.

He called Ray "Pops." Sneered at Wilkie as he and his fat buddy passed by their table inside the Sloppy's next door to the coffee bar.

The cooler was full of designer salads that all looked sad and wilted.

Wilkie suddenly cursed himself for leaving the phone in his pocket. Ray had told him to make as much video as he could. It would show the world just how the kids crumbled in the face of true adversity. Show them how they needed a place like Oakridge Academy.

Wilkie had the idea that the world was too far from redemption. Society had long ago moved beyond the desire to learn.

He pulled the KyMera camera out of his pocket. Took a moment to admire how the camera was able to pick up so much detail with such little light. A combination of a large sensor and AI baked into the phone. Aimed the camera through the gap in the boards as Ty came creeping by. Ignoring his surroundings in favor of staring into his own camera.

"I can't just leave 'em behind," he hissed. "Y'all know what I went through to get these. Episode seven hundred? The one that finally got me over the hundred thousand mark?"

Wilkie glanced up to see the number of views the Operation: Gen Z stream was getting. Over nine hundred thousand. It was hard to believe that so many people were just sitting in front of a screen. Watching the same thing.

He had argued about how millions of people tuning into football was no different, but Ray told him he was wrong. Something about binge-watching and digital delivery and something else that Wilkie had stopped paying attention to.

It didn't feel any different to him. Most of America tuning into the last episode of *M*A*S*H* or a championship game or a livestream where dumb fuck kids got murdered.

So many people wasting so much time. Instead of watching football, I play it. Instead of watching a murder …

He grinned at his own joke.

At the truck stop, he had finished watching the kid and

his fat buddy stroll away like they had won a championship fight. Looked back at Ray to see him nod. Just once. Permission to do something Wilkie hadn't even asked for.

Ray had just known. Like always.

Wilkie stood. Usually, he tried to stoop a little. Pull his shoulders in. He hated the attention he usually got. The stares. Pointing fingers.

Ray had told him it was just because people weren't used to seeing somebody in such a state of physical superiority. He was only a specimen.

It still made him feel like a freak. Wishing he could be *normal*.

Until he saw the fear on the fat buddy's face. The way he made other men feel when he stood up to his full height. The way his piggy eyes widened when he saw Wilkie's fist coming so fast, he could never get out of the way.

Bone breaking under his knuckles. Blood slicking his skin.

There was only one stall door closed, so Wilkie grabbed the sagging body and picked him up. At the satisfaction of lifting the fat shit up so easily, he welcomed the stares, only there was nobody else in the restroom.

He threw the body, and the stall door exploded into the stall, crushing the smug fucker under the metal's weight, plus the three hundred pounds of blubber that — up to this point — he'd always called a friend.

Wilkie bent into the smell of the kid's final thought hitting the bowl beneath him. Stopped to pull the shiny hunting knife from the sheath on the belt now hanging at the kid's ankles.

The pudgy bastard on top bled in a slow trickle when he dragged the blade across his throat, but the kid struggling to get his pants back up made a jet Wilkie had to dodge. Side-stepping the spray and jumping back out of the stall.

He washed his hands. Dried the knife under the blower. When he left the restroom he pulled the cleaning cart in front of the door. Returned to his seat so he could finish his True American with extra cheese and no onions.

Ray didn't ask what happened. Such was the trust he had in him. When they left, Wilkie walked out with his chest proud, and his head high.

Let them stare.

"You needy motherfucker," Ty said. "Like you know what's gonna happen."

Wilkie tried not to laugh. With every other step sounding like taco night, tracking him was going to be easy as chocolate pie.

"Fine." Ty held the phone out so his audience could watch him take his shoes off. Held them over his head while he eased his feet down on the mossy growth with a frown of distaste.

"Aw fuck. It's cold as shit." Stared at the comments. "No, I ain't gonna leave 'em. Too dope to just let 'em go. Especially sitting in the swamp that's growing outta this carpet."

Wilkie drew a deep breath, then burst from his hiding place with a growl.

Ty screamed as he pinwheeled his arms and fell back, his precious shoes flying from his fingers. Before Wilkie could capitalize on Ty's surprise, he paused to let the laughter die.

The look of naked shock on the kid's face had lit in his mind like comedy neon. A sign that told him to keep laughing. A problem he'd had for years. Even Matheson locking him in the dark for weeks at a time couldn't keep the giggles at bay.

Wilkie made an effort to move toward Ty as he caught his breath, but the kid was long gone. Just depressions in the sodden carpet where his toes had pushed him into a sprint.

The *slap slap* of wet socks. Then silence.

Wilkie shook his head. Brought the knife up to jab into the skin under his chin. Deep enough to penetrate. Draw blood. Enough to stop his uncontrollable laughter.

He held the blade to his own throat as he raised the phone. Scrolled away from his own feed to stop on Ty's video.

Darkness brightened by flashes of his teeth as he whispered to his followers. "What the fuck was that shit? I ain't trying to die from no Swamp Thing-looking motherfucker."

Wilkie moved into the hallway next to the stairs. Into the first door. Plenty of things to hide behind.

"I'm gonna stay right here under this desk until he's gone."

Wilkie didn't see any desks, so he turned to go into the door across the hall.

Ty's eyes widened, then pressed closed as he tucked his chin down and waited. Holding his breath.

Wilkie didn't bother being quiet. Instead, he stomped as he moved to the desk. A growl that started deep in his chest and rose into a ragged scream as he set the phone down and bent to reach for Ty's neck.

Pulled him up by the throat. Lifted him to hang, kicking and struggling in front of him.

He didn't drop his phone until Wilkie drove the knife into his guts just under his breastbone. Pulled the serrated blade out in a splash of blood and stomach acid.

When he lowered Ty to his feet, the kid remained standing. Hands over his pumping wound. Bright smile dulled by blood covering his teeth. Eyes staring at something far away from the pain.

Wilkie picked up Ty's phone. Held it out so the camera had a nice view. It had no problem showing the slash that cut so deep, Ty's head flopped back on the remaining flesh at the back of his neck. White bone gleaming from the wound as the body fell back to spasm with the spots of oxygen still in the muscles as it died.

Wilkie set the phone on Ty's chest, and noticed the feed was over one million.

Chapter Sixteen

Craig caught up with Kat as she followed Jeff into a room just past the intersection.

Jeff bent to the floor. Grabbed a board. Threw it over his shoulder. A scrap of cloth. A cracked broom handle.

Kat moved back until her back was pressed against the wall. "What are you doing?"

Jeff glanced back. Looked from Kat to Craig. "Trying to find something Ira can grab."

Craig had to take a moment to realize Jeff was really trying to help. He wasn't just running away like he had. He nodded and dropped to his hands and knees. "Yeah, something we can pull him up with."

There was nothing in the debris in front of him except for glass and splinters hiding in the gritty filth.

Kat held her hands over her head. "Wait!"

Craig froze at her shout. Watched Jeff drop into a holding position. Looking at her with his eyebrows climbing. Craig was struck by how frightened he looked.

"I heard something," Kat whispered.

A crashing some distance away in the hallway outside the room. Kat pointed. "There!"

Craig rose up and leaned back to peer around the edge of the doorway. Two shapes struggling through the mountain of garbage. Weaving and stumbling.

He stood up and stepped out for a better look.

"No, Craig!" Kat hissed.

Craig held his hand up to her and shook his head. "Hang on."

The two figures hit a flat spot. Got some speed, even though clinging to each other had to be slowing them down. Then Craig recognized them. "Holy shit! It's Selena and Marcy."

Jeff was at his side. Craig wondered if he would have been there as quickly had it been Oz and Kelly.

When the girls stepped into the meager light coming out of the intersection, Craig saw the blood.

Slashes across Selena's face. Down Marcy's arms. Crimson soaking the fronts of their shirts. Matting down their hair.

They looked up at the same time. Saw Craig and Jeff, and their faces collapsed into desperate relief. They all tumbled back into the room in a tangle of arms. Marcy weeping into Craig's ear. Selena's voice a long run-on sentence.

"There's a zombie after us with a knife and she cut my face my face she cut us and chased us what am I going to do she cut my face—"

Craig pulled Marcy away from Selena. Put her back in the corner and stood in front of her. Looked up into her eyes.

But her gaze was fixed on the space behind his head.

He shook her shoulders. "Marcy!"

She blinked. Wiped her cheeks dry, leaving smears of blood in place of the tears. "What?"

Craig took her hands. "What happened?"

She shook her head. "I don't know. We found the auditorium. Right to it like no problem, right? We were going to win, but the doors were locked."

Craig lifted her hands up and looked down at the dripping slashes on her arms. "Honey, what happened to your arms?"

She looked down like it was the first time she had seen them. "Oh. The zombie came out of the room across the hall from the auditorium, you know? She was screaming. Covered in … it was awful. She cut Selena's face. She's beautiful. Did you know that?"

Craig nodded. "Everybody knew that. Then what happened?"

Marcy shrugged. "We ran. Do you have a tissue?"

Kat stepped up to him. Took Marcy's hands. "Come on, sweetie. I have some."

Marcy smiled. "Oh, good."

She took Marcy to where Selena sat on top of a stack of damp cardboard. "… and she just came out and cut me and Marcy and she was screaming and she cut my face and in the camera I could see the bone underneath and she cut me …"

Craig turned away from the girls' circle and found Jeff standing next to him.

"A zombie?" Jeff asked.

Craig shrugged. "That's what Marcy said."

"Zombies usually don't attack with knives."

"Well, you might be surprised to know that zombies aren't real."

"Maybe, but they certainly believe."

Craig rolled his eyes. "So *we* should start believing in zombies, too? Next, you'll tell me fairies are real."

Jeff grinned as he indicated Craig with a tip of his head. "Aren't they?"

"Fuck you."

Jeff chuckled. "All I'm saying is that's what they said they saw."

"Really? A *zombie*?"

"No, probably a meth head. Or a hobo scared out of his refrigerator box. Or somebody *dressed* as a zombie."

"But why?"

Jeff shrugged. "I don't know. But why lure a bunch of kids into an old school to kill 'em one by one?"

"For views, I guess." Craig didn't like being this close to Jeff. Maybe had it been in different circumstances. Hanging at his house and sitting next to Angel at the dinner table. He shook his head to banish the thought. "So, what now?"

"We either have to find some rope or something to pull Ira through the hole, or find a way to get to him and … I don't know. Dig him out? *Break* him out?"

"No!" Selena shouted.

Jeff and Craig turned to find her on her feet. She threw her hair over her shoulder and blood flew from the gaping cuts across her cheek. A glint of fat and bone and his stomach tightened.

The burning ham from the MRE rose into his throat. He looked away and forced it back down.

"You have to leave," Selena said. "You all have to leave!"

Kat stood up next to her. "But what about the money?"

Craig felt a wave of ice roll up from his legs. Shocked disappointment. If she had asked about Ira instead, he would have followed her to the edges of the Earth.

Jeff stepped forward. "We have to find something to get Ira out first."

Craig's head whipped around so he could look at Jeff in disbelief. He had said the thing Craig wished Kat had said. Could he believe what he saw and heard anymore?

"You guys are crazy if you think you can win. It's not for people like you. It's for people like *us*." Selena grabbed Marcy's shirt and pulled her up. Marcy struggled to her feet, standing next to Selena with her chin jutting out in defiance.

"*We're* the ones," Selena continued. "We *deserve* this. We're pretty ..." One hand came up to trail through the air right in front of her facial wounds. "We're the pretty ones."

Marcy nodded. "We're going to win."

Craig waited for somebody else to say something as Selena turned toward Marcy and pulled her into a hug. Like sisters holding onto each other at a funeral. Something felt off about them. He wasn't sure if this was how competitive and singlemindedly focused on being the "pretty ones" they'd always been or if they were so shook by what happened that they'd latched onto these things as both drive and denial.

He threw his hands up in frustration. "What about the zombie?"

Marcy shook her head. "You said it yourself. Zombies aren't real."

Kat put her hands on her hips. "Then who cut your face, you dumbass?"

Marcy shook her head as she burrowed into Selena's hair with a whisper, "We're the pretty ones."

"We're the pretty ones," Selena repeated, almost robotically.

Kat looked at Craig in disbelief. He wasn't ready to meet her gaze.

Craig turned to Jeff. "So, how about that rope?"

Jeff nodded his head like he was thinking about something else. "Yeah. We should totally go get some rope or something."

When Kat reached for Selena, Marcy pulled her away. Turned so their backs were away from her. Kat pulled her hand back as if bitten. Walked over to Craig with her head down. Even now, it was hard for her to be spurned by the pretty girls.

She had often told him about her fear that she would never be good enough. Pretty enough. For most of the boys at school, or even in life. Boys like Jeff.

He knew exactly how she felt. And though Jeff was clearly an asshole, Craig had to admit it came from a deep sadness. The knowledge that Jeff was only a villain because Craig couldn't have him. The feeling that he could *never* have a boy like Jeff. Then he blushed with shame. Ira wasn't a boy like Jeff, but he was certainly a boy Craig didn't deserve.

Craig held his arm out, and Kat slid up against him. Best friends again.

He wondered if she would still be his best friend if they made it to the auditorium.

Chapter Seventeen

Ira waited until he couldn't hear them anymore. Just his own breathing echoing back to him from the dusty walls. Then he got to exploring. Humming "Megalovania" while swiping at the glowing motes of dust.

Just in case his body cam had audio.

He hadn't jumped on the *Undertale* bandwagon like many of his friends. He was too busy with *GTA:V* and *Minecraft*. But when the indie RPG finally came to his Nintendo Switch, Ira realized how much fun he had been missing out on.

It had started cutting into his *Among Us* time. Then the updated *No Man's Sky* had come out. He shook his head as he let the *Undertale* song fade away. "There's just not enough time, guys."

He climbed over an unsteady pile of debris covered by the damp fall of carpet that had cushioned his landing. Dropped to the sweating concrete in the corner. Pulled the tattered tail of carpet up. Sneered in disgust at the rusty smear of grime covering rotting cardboard boxes.

He let the carpet drop back down and wiped his hands on the front of his shirt. "And I'm still young. Just a kid according to Ray. Our bus driver. Probably the guy trying to kill us."

He climbed back up to look at the hole in the ceiling.

"Isn't that weird? I won a contest ... well, not even that. The *chance* to be in a contest."

He turned in a slow circle. Ended up facing a set of shelves leaning against the wall. Covered in a crust of whatever was in the jars and cans that had fallen along with it. Broken glass and dented metal.

He made his way over the treacherous footing.

"And what would have happened when we got there, guys? Would we have turned on each other to be the first to tap the plate without new phones?"

He froze at the sight of something he'd missed.

"Hey, it's a door."

He placed his foot on a flat spot next to a weeping paint can. Leaned to the side to see the shelf had fallen against an old steel door, pitted with rust and chemical scaling.

He put his hands on the cleanest spot he could find. Pushed with a grunt, but the shelf barely moved. Like it was welded to the wall.

He dropped his head when he started crying. Realized there was nobody down here to see him cry. He looked down at the body cam. The audience couldn't see his face, but he kept speaking, hoping it was going to viewers instead of some psycho looking to kill him.

But maybe he could get some sympathy from the psychos?

"Who am I doing this for? It's damn sure not for me."

He let his hands fall. Made his way back to the center of the room to look up at the ceiling once more.

"I've never done *anything* for myself. Except for the gaming. That was just for me cuz nobody else in my family understands it. But I love it, and the only way I can do it is if I do everything *they* want — the grades and the extra credit and the job fairs and …"

He crossed his arms. Realized he had covered the camera. Sighed as he put his hands in his pockets to keep the view clear.

"My mom gets it a little. At least the money, right? I'll be honest, guys. The channel's doing alright. The merch. Patreon. All of it. My only concern when coming out was how it might affect my views. The number of subscribers."

His laugh sounded hoarse. Throat burning from crying to a bunch of people who didn't give a single shit about him. A thousand other streamers ready to jump into the gap if he quit … or died.

"My family cared about me as much as I provided for them. Which is to say, more and more every day, but not *quite* enough. All I ever wanted was for somebody to love me for who I was, and not for what I could give them."

A fresh bark of laughter caught Ira by surprise. The sad humor in his situation made him shake his head. Wiping the tears from his cheeks on the backs of his fists.

"The only person who did seem to love me … I pushed him away. What a dumbass."

Ira wished he had his phone so he could see the comments. Get that sweet validation. Not feel so alone.

A noise up in the hall above him made him catch his breath. Look up to squint into the ragged hole.

A sound behind him, and he spun around to see what it was. Nothing there.

He heard it again. Like something in the walls.

Dust sifted down from the hole. He shielded his eyes to look back up. Saw a shape at the edge of the light. He lifted a hand. Smiled as he opened his mouth to shout, but something made him hesitate.

The scurrying sound of something in the walls again. Then a loud squeal of protesting metal. The weight of the heavy shelf moving as the old door growled open.

Ira backed away, and his feet tangled on the unsure surface of the lumpy carpet. He fell back and kept retreating in a crab walk that left his back soaking wet from dragging across the dank floor.

The door hit the shelf, making it rattle. The door closed and opened again, harder.

For a moment the shelf teetered, like it might fight gravity and remain upright.

No such luck.

It came crashing down. Jars and cans jumbling into a pile that sounded like when the recyclers emptied his can every Wednesday.

His mom drank a bottle of wine a day. His older brother contributed a few cases of Milwaukee's Best. The crash and tinkle of the cans and bottles emptying into the back of the recycling truck was embarrassing.

Ira pulled his feet up to keep the acrid splash of paint and chemicals off his shoes. Felt the sting of fumes in the air before breathing it in and doubling over with a gagging cough.

He looked up through watering eyes to see a monster standing in the hall outside the door. Taller and wider than the opening. Covered in vines and dead grass like it emerged from some dirty lake.

Ira held his breath. Looked in the only direction he remembered had a way out. Up to the ceiling.

In the hole was a face. A pleasant smile that calmed him, even as he heard the lake monster come into the room.

"Well, hello there, kid," Ray said.

Chapter Eighteen

Scheherazade continued to follow the clues. From the wooden cross made from fence slats leading her down the side yard to the broken window, to the plastic hatchet in the filing cabinet.

While arguing with the dipshits about who she really was if not Alicia Brown. Except for Craig. He'd figured out who she was, but that made sense. He was more interested in identity than the rest.

Except maybe for the jock. He had the look of somebody still trying to figure out who he was. Still finding his place in the world.

Craig had said he knew her secret, but if so he never said it. Not so she could hear it, anyway. Of course, his hint had led the viewers right to her. They were calling her by her screen name in no time.

N0BLE

The hacker alias she had used since figuring out her neighbor's wifi password at seven years old. Using their bandwidth to travel the world.

Nobody knew that N0BLE was Schae Gardner,

though. Unless Craig blurted out her real name. Then a lot of people would be able to put two and two together.

She wouldn't have to hide her true identity much longer anyway. She was planning to ditch it for a new assumed life the second she was done at Oakridge. After she found her grandfather.

An old master sergeant back in Vietnam, everyone — including the grandkids — called him Top. And he was in trouble.

She could still feel his old leathery hands on the back of her neck as he led her through another treasure hunt in the backyard.

"You need a reference point, girl. Somewhere to start from." His voice sounded like thick smoke and brambles.

The hunts always started with a zero. A clue to the next point. Direction and distance. All she had to do was follow the clues to the prize. A stuffed bunny or a Pez dispenser full of candy.

As long as she had a place to start.

Even before finding the wooden cross, she'd had a starting point with Top's last letter. He told her about Oakridge Academy. About how he was afraid to come out of hiding. Terrified of something he wouldn't name.

She had assumed it was KyMera, but it turned out Karen Beal's company had little to do with the contest anyway. They were just a sponsor. Staking into it for data and social clout.

A confused web of small companies — mostly e-commerce and local businesses rising to affiliate with a tech juggernaut. It was easy for Schae to fix the contest so Jackson High would win.

Alicia Brown was too rich. Too beautiful. Too stuck-up to lower herself to enter a contest that her daddy could buy three times over. What she really needed was followers. Views. Virtual adoration.

Schae offered her a deal. A hundred thousand — *real* — subscribers to her LiveLyfe channel in exchange for her spot on the bus.

Even a person with everything could be bought.

The hardest part was losing the fifteen pounds to look more like Alicia. Schae couldn't count on going unnoticed just by being Black. In truth, she had been constantly terrified of discovery. As Craig had pointed out when he'd finally seen her face, she looked nothing like Alicia Brown.

Sitting in front of a computer all day had done more to ruin her health — and her figure — than the pizza and Bang! energy drinks. The promise she made to herself to take better care of her body once this was all over was repeated daily, but being so out of breath told her the contest couldn't have happened soon enough.

She ducked into the shadows under the eave of a large wood shed under the cover of dripping limbs. Water, pine tar, and falling needles making a gentle shower on the cedar shake roof.

Top had given her the clues she needed to get into Operation: Gen Z — the dumbest name of any contest she had ever heard. Once at Oakridge, he had given her a starting point. A wooden cross made from fence slats that didn't match anything else she had seen on the property. One of the arms sharpened to a point, aimed at the rear corner of the building.

It led her to the fence leaning against the wall like a ladder leading up to the broken window. Made from the same wood as the cross.

It had taken her far too long to find that first clue. Hiding so soon after she started when the arrows flew out of the trees and caught Malcolm and Mia on fire.

Top's letter had taken on more urgent importance in her mind as she had huddled under the cover of an overturned refrigerator that smelled like burned dog fur. Sobbing while trying to avoid stepping into her own vomit.

Then she found the plastic hatchet.

Top had always carried a real one on a loop hanging from his belt. The handle stained by years of sweat. The aged metal oiled and sharpened to a shining line along the edge. A hammer head opposite the blade.

He'd once upon a time taken her to the woodshed. Handed the small hatchet to her. Let her pick out a nice piece of wood. Carefully shave off a chunk large enough for the project, and they would sit together under the tree and whittle. Her first effort had been a duck. Lumpy and crooked, but Top had beamed. Promised to keep it always.

When those boys had hurt Erin … Schae remembered seeing Top's face when they brought her sister home from the hospital. The way the skin tightened around his eyes. The way she thought she would never again see him smile.

He told her to sit tight. Told her it might be a minute before she saw him again. She watched him go to the shed. Saw the hatchet bouncing from his hip when he left.

Those boys never hurt anyone ever again, and Schae hadn't seen Top since. But he wrote. A letter a month, and she took to computers to try and find him. Once she did, she was old enough to know why she could never tell. Why she could never go to him.

The plastic hatchet led her to the woodshed. She knew he wouldn't be inside. It was still too exposed. Too easy to be discovered living inside. And now that she saw what he was hiding from, it made sense.

There would be another clue.

She wiped her hands on her legs. Stepped out of the

shade to squeeze through the opening of the old crooked door stuck in the tall weeds.

The interior was a dim jumble of shapes. Schae pulled out her phone. Navigated by the light glow from her screen.

A pile of soaked and rotting wood half covered with a tattered blue tarp. Covered in smears of raccoon droppings. A sagging workbench along the wall. Cabinets with no doors and rusty contents. A stinging scent of feral animals. Sticky air that made her exposed skin feel grimy and cold.

She glanced down at the screen. Smiled at the feed from Alicia's profile. A static shot from where she had strapped her body cam to the back of a chair. Aimed at a blackboard with some bullshit written on it.

New chalk, and carefully lettered.

TRAIN UP A CHILD IN THE WAY HE SHOULD GO,

AND WHEN HE IS OLD HE WILL NOT DEPART FROM IT.

Something some angry Boomer would say.

She paused in surprise when she saw the viewer count pass a million. So many blind people in spite of their eyes showing them the truth.

She turned the screen around and directed her gaze back to her search, but it wasn't long before she saw the next clue. A small stuffed bunny perched on top of a dented can of deck stain. Far too clean for its surroundings.

She picked it up. Gave it a squeeze and pulled it up to her nose for a breath. It smelled like him. Pine and vanilla. The salve he used to keep his hands from cracking.

She smiled into the bunny's fur. Asked herself where it could have come from.

Where did rabbits live?

A den? A warren? A hutch?

She stuffed the little guy into her jacket before going out to look for the next clue.

The sun was low. Behind her was the remaining light of the day. In front of her was night made darker by rolling clouds. Instead of the sound of dripping leaves, she heard the sound of actual rain. Distant thunder. It made it hard to hear anybody sneaking up on her, but it also made *her* harder to hear.

Sneaking around in the dark. Trained up as a child by a dear old man who now needed her. She wasn't *that* up on the Bible, but hopefully, Proverbs was right.

Chapter Nineteen

Craig thought he heard voices. Other footsteps. Weird doppler echoes of sound. But what he thought was static turned out to be rain.

Faint at first, it built into a blanket of noise that made him want to shout everything to be heard. Then heavy dripping as the water infiltrated the failing structure. Dribbling and splashing and spreading within minutes of starting.

Most of the doors were locked or blocked. The ones that opened showed more of the same. Old classrooms. Trash. Graffiti and damage. Chalk drawings of dicks and Bible verses on the blackboards in equal measure.

Out of the main hallway they found a dank set of stairs next to a small utility closet. Craig stayed outside as Jeff and Kat went into the dark, but Kat soon popped her head back out. "I can't see, and my phone is ... dirty."

She had left it in a puddle of her own puke, but whatever. He handed her the lighter he had found in the first room. She struck it alight and turned to continue her search, but Jeff pushed her back into the hall.

"*Put it out!*" he hissed.

Her face became defiant, and she put her hand on her hip. Before she could say anything, Craig reached up and snapped the lid closed. She turned her anger on him, but Jeff pushed between them with a small red can of gasoline.

"I just don't wanna explode."

Kat pulled her head in. Bared her teeth in alarm as her gaze followed the can to the floor as Jeff set it down. "What's in it?"

Craig expected Jeff to give them some smartass comment, but instead he said, "I think it's a two-stroke mixture. You know, gas and oil for small stuff like weed whackers and leaf blowers. It smells fresh too."

Craig handed his phone to Kat. She returned his lighter with a guilty smile. Ducked back into the closet to keep looking.

"We just need a bottle or something," Jeff said.

Craig stared at the red gas can. "For what?"

"What do they call 'em? Molotov cocktails? I always put 'em on my wheel in *GTA*. Sticky bombs and mines. Usually, I can even get 'em all the way up in the air to take the helicopters out whenever I get five stars."

"The fuck are you talking about?"

Jeff shook his head like he was trying to clear away a dream. "*Grand Theft Auto*. You never played it? Bro, the online stuff is tremendous."

"Ira showed me some of it, but I'm not that familiar. I don't really game at all, to be honest."

Kat emerged with an old boombox. Stained gray plastic the size of a suitcase. "It works."

"You plugged it in?" Craig asked.

"No, it has batteries."

"What kind? A car battery? It's the size of your Honda."

Jeff dismissed the boombox. "You see any bottles?"

Kat nodded. "Blue ones." She set the boombox down and turned back.

Craig watched her bend down and grab something from the floor. A spark of blue light reflecting from sapphires in her hands.

"You want that to save Ira, right?"

She ignored his dig.

Jeff straightened with his bat back up on his shoulder. "Whatever happened to every man for himself?"

Craig looked up at him and squared his shoulders. "Ty said that, not me. We're in this together, as far as I'm concerned."

"Are we?" Jeff asked. "Because you've been kind of an asshole to me this whole trip."

"You've been a total dick to me since the second grade."

"Are you serious right now?"

"Always picking on me and my friends."

"I've never picked on *anybody*."

"Bullshit."

"When? What have I *ever* said to you?"

"Nothing. That's the point."

Jeff blinked like he was trying to come awake. "What am I missing here?"

Craig laughed. "That figures. Just hangin' out with your bully asshole friends. Letting them treat people like me like shit."

"*Letting* them? What are you talking about?"

"Craig." Kat handed the blue bottle to Jeff. Put her hand on Craig's shoulder. "I don't think you're being fair."

Craig shrugged her hand away. "That's only because I'm saying it about your secret crush."

She pulled her hand back. Stared at him with wide glistening eyes. Mouth falling open.

He told himself to stop. Knew if he said any more, he would never be able to go back. He also knew there was no use. "He's your Golden Boy. Mr. Perfect. You've always defended him, even though he could have done something a thousand times to keep Malcolm, or one of his caveman asshole friends, from saying horrible things or doing horrible things or just …"

Jeff lowered the bat. Leaned it against the wall. "Let me get this straight. It's not enough that I never said or *did* anything to you, I also had to keep everybody else from doing or saying shit too? I had to be some moral policeman so you never had to deal with other people's crap?"

Kat hugged herself as she stepped back into the closet like she was trying to hide. "What's wrong with you?"

Jeff grinned. "I get it. You're mad because I never asked you out. Is that it? I'm not *her* secret crush. I'm *yours*."

Craig bit his lip. Started to deny it. Filled his chest with air so he could shout it down. Then the wind hissed through his teeth and he was looking through the distortion of tears. "Yes," he said.

Years of looking at himself in the mirror and hating what he saw. Wishing he could be more like the kids that everybody liked.

The ones that seemed to never have any trouble. The ones that always seemed happy.

Secretly staring at Jeff from the corner. The way he moved. His smile. Until Malcolm had called Craig a "fucking faggot," and Jeff's smile had no longer seemed so beautiful.

It was dark and evil and represented how everyone who didn't understand him looked at him.

He had been furious with Jeff. Not because he couldn't have him, but because Jeff's smile had ruined the fantasy. He had confirmed that Craig *never* had a chance with him, but at least before the smile he could have *pretended*.

"Oh, Craig," Kat whispered. She was in his arms, and he was crying on her shoulder. Maybe it was the stress of the contest. Or years of repressed pain. Or bad ham from an MRE.

He wept like a baby, and Kat held him. He was aware of Jeff watching him. Standing silently. Forced to share in a private moment.

Craig pushed away from Kat and wiped his eyes. Took a deep breath before looking up at Jeff, but before he could say anything, Jeff held up his hand.

"I don't owe you shit. And it's fucked up that you assumed I wasn't going to help. But I am. And I'm sorry."

Craig didn't want his apology. He just wanted to pretend none of this had ever happened. "For what?"

"For not doing more? I don't know. I broke Cameron Holstead's ribs for calling Angel a retard once, but she's my sister, and the greatest person I know. Sorry to say it, but you were just a kid from school."

"Exactly," Craig sighed, and he saw the moment when Jeff finally got it.

Jeff blinked and leaned away. "Oh."

Craig had only ever wanted to be more than *just a kid from school*.

Jeff grabbed the bat. Stooped for the boombox as he cleared his throat. "If you get the gas can, Katherine can carry the bottle for me."

Kat smiled and looked down at her feet. "You can call me Kat."

Craig ignored her batting eyelashes. "What for?"

Jeff looked into Craig's eyes and smiled. "We're gonna do what Ira said. Squad mode, remember?"

Craig saw that smile he remembered from years ago. Back when he thought about what it would have felt like to be the reason for it. "And then what?"

"I have a plan." Jeff's smile became a full grin, and Craig was jealous of every girl that would ever see it.

To distract himself from the flush filling his face, Craig reached out for his phone. Kat dropped it into his hand, then he opened the screen and navigated to Ira's feed.

He put his hand over his mouth when he saw it was just a black rectangle.

Then the black became lighter shadows. Then snatches of light and color, finally resolving into somebody stepping away. The sound of a soft moan.

Leaves and vines swaying as the monster that killed Oz and Kelly moved out of frame. Another moan.

The camera was pointed at an open door. A figure beyond it moved in the darkness, weaving between falling streams of water.

Ray ducked through the doorway. Looked at Ira, seeming to somehow meet Craig's gaze through the camera. The murdering leaf monster came back into view. Set a camp chair down before kneeling on the floor. As Ray sat down with a groan, a wisp of smoke curled around the monster's shoulders. Then light danced behind his frame.

He stood up, and the light of a campfire burned the image out. Craig closed the phone. Slid it back in his pocket. Took a few deep breaths before saying anything.

The smell of wood smoke was oddly calming.

"What's your plan now?" he said.

Chapter Twenty

Ray adjusted his position in the chair. The wet was making his old joints ache. Especially his lower back. Or maybe it was the cancer eating away at his insides.

He smiled as he pulled a cigar out of the hard case in his cargo pocket. A Perdomo Champagne Epicure.

Whenever he got a young man started on cigars, this was the one he gave them. Not much power, but a lot of flavor, and it stayed lit. A good one to use to impress them with the experience of cigar smoking.

When the doctor had told him he would only last a month if he didn't seek treatment — a young man who treated Ray like he was stupid for getting cancer in the first place — Ray had gone out and bought two boxes. One cigar a day would mean he had plenty of cigars for the rest of his life.

Six months later, he was still alive. On his fifth box.

Not long now, though.

His cutter had cost eighty dollars. A job was only as good as the tools a man used. Medical-grade stainless that held its edge so it cut the tobacco instead of crushing it. A triple flame torch to toast the foot before touching the fire to it and drawing.

A gentle pull. Rotating the stick in his mouth. Watching the flame leap with each puff.

He put the lighter back. Blew on the burning coal at the end of the cigar. Took his first true draw. Watched Ira's eyes glitter with reflected firelight through the billow of smoke.

The kid's hands were tied together and looped over a hook screwed into the stud under the crumbling plaster of the far wall. One of those orange utility hooks for storing ladders up off the garage floor.

He stared with a fearless intensity that Ray could find respect for. A man faced with reality willing to look into the abyss was a rarity.

He nodded in confirmation of the bravery Ira had managed to find at the end. Smiled when Ira nodded back.

Wilkie distracted him by dropping down next to the fire with a can of beans he fished out from under his ghillie suit. Opened it with the huge knife he got at the truck stop. Looked like it still had blood on it.

Ray felt for the small knife he had found under the floor in the coat room. Relaxed at the feel of its outline through the fabric of his pants.

He took another pull from the cigar. Pointed the smoking foot at Ira. "You know the problem with your generation? You have no understanding of people."

Ray shifted his attention from Ira's face to the camera strapped to his bony chest.

"You see the world only as a reflection of yourselves. Everything is only and always about ... *you*."

He took his phone and set it on the floor next to him. Popped the little kickstand out. Aimed it by eye so it was pointing at Ira. "How great and important you are, and how wrong everyone else is."

He leaned back for another draw. Tipped his head back to blow the smoke up toward the cracked ceiling. "This generation thinks they're the first ones to stand up for something, but it's just words. Nothing but air and shouting into the wind."

He rolled the edge of the ash on the metal sticking out of the fraying fabric on the arm of the chair. "*We* did it through action. We never talked about how great we were, or the measure of our worth in likes and followers. We showed up and did something about the things we saw wrong with the world."

Ira sniffed. "You're the ones who *made* the world what it is."

Ray stood up. Made sure not to grunt or moan, even as the pain in his hips made him swallow the acid rising in his throat. "Is that right? And what exactly is it that you think we have done? And be specific if you can."

Ira stared through falling tears.

Ray nodded. "I understand. Your generation deals in concepts and emotion. Not so much in facts."

He closed the distance between them, making sure his phone on the floor still had a clear shot. "Do you know why this contest is called Operation: Gen Z? A lot of comments said the name was stupid, and maybe they were right, but only because I'm sure they thought the *Gen Z* was for *Generation Z* — after all, everything is about *you*. But no, the true meaning of the name is *Operation General Zaroff*, from *The Most Dangerous Game*."

He stared into Ira's face. Smiled and nodded his head when he saw no recognition there. "I figured as much. So let me educate you. It was a short story written in 1924." He held up his hand like Ira had protested. "It was also a movie in 1932. I know your generation doesn't much care for reading. And there are many other movies and shows based on it, but, as is often the case, nothing beats the original."

He paused to gather his thoughts. Blew a cloud of smoke to circle Ira's head. "General Zaroff hunted humans. Because he was bored. But I'm doing it because I'm a man of action. I see a problem in the world, I *do* something about it."

He bent to retrieve a piece of bent metal from the floor. Turned it over and looked along its length. Grinned at the fear he saw in Ira's eyes.

He brought the bar to the fire. Poked it to get the flames up. "Matheson said we would all be too late. That the change was happening. It was inexorable. Inevitable. A matter of momentum. And I should have listened to him. I'm too late to change anything, but there are others out there that might be able to make the changes I can't. They just need a push. Something to show them the way to go. *Someone* to show them. Like General Zaroff was to me, so I can be to others. An inspiration."

The cigar was half gone. A straight even burn. Perfect construction. Quality in every way. Like how it used to be. "You know, Karen Beal wanted to call it Operation Z. She's not as young as you, but she's younger than me, and much like the current generation, she has no memory for the past. Operation Z was the name of the Japanese plan to protect the Marianas." He turned to point his cigar at Ira again. "The planning for the attack on Pearl Harbor. A blow to the Americans so great, we would be forced to end the war. Of course, the men of the time — men of action like me — put an end to the war in a completely different way, but who remembers the mistakes of the past? To her credit, Karen Beal listened when I told her. Something I can never say for you and your fellow Zoomers. Youth needs to learn to listen to experience."

"Yeah?" Ira said, his voice cracking. Trailing into a wheeze as he took a deep breath. Cleared his throat. "Maybe *you* should try listening to us!"

Ray threw his head back and laughed. Wilkie snorted into his can of beans. "You have absolutely nothing to teach me, son. But whether you believe it or not, I gotta couple things to show *you*."

He paused when he heard something. He tipped his ear up as he took another draw from his cigar. Let the smoke trickle out.

Music. He closed his eyes. Almost had the name of the song. He just couldn't quite get it. Wilkie distracted him by throwing his can aside and standing up.

Ray tossed the last inch of his cigar into the fire. "At least they're doing something. Maybe taking a stand. Good for them." He tipped his head toward the door. "Go find out what they're doing."

Wilkie nodded his shaggy head and stomped out.

Ray stood in front of Ira. Watched him try to be strong even as tears spilled down his cheeks. Ray reached up and hooked his fingers through the collar of Ira's shirt. Made a fist and jerked down to tear a strip out of the shirt that exposed Ira's chest, rolling the body cam down to his waist.

He could see his heart pounding so hard it made his ribs vibrate like something was trying to escape him. Ray pulled the knife out. Opened the rusty blade. Touched it to the hollow of Ira's throat. "What would you like me to listen to?"

Chapter Twenty-One

Craig followed Jeff deeper into the building. He didn't bother looking at his phone to see where the auditorium target was. He didn't believe it even existed.

Instead, he held Kat's hand as they jogged through the dripping hallway.

"Here we go," Jeff said. "This should work."

They entered a gym. Wooden parquet floor curling up like flakes of shredded coconut. Sagging bleachers collapsing into soggy piles.

Water dripped from the center of the high ceiling to make a small puddle in the center of a trampoline surrounded by a berm of rotting cushions and wrestling mats.

"Cool," Kat whispered.

Craig looked at the appreciation on her face. "This place? I mean, I can see why *he* likes it. The place where *sportsball* was born. But *you*?"

She pointed at the trampoline. "It's the *Halo* Moment."

"What?"

"If they try to shoot us with a burning arrow, we can

just jump around. Like Ira said, it makes you harder to hit."

Jeff shook his head. "You'd probably go right through. Into a pit of spikes or something. Like in *Rambo*."

Craig led Kat past the trampoline to stand under the basketball backboard at the far end of the room. "There was a trampoline in *Rambo*?"

Jeff set the boombox on the floor. "What? No, the spikes. Like in the tunnel when the drug dealers came?"

Craig shrugged. "I never saw that movie."

"Now what?" Kat said.

Jeff turned the speakers of the boombox to face the door. "I turn this on. Crank it up. Pour some gas in the bottle. Hide in a hole in the bleachers and throw this on anybody that shows up. Gimme that lighter."

Craig handed it over without comment. Jeff nodded. Then he dropped to look at the front of the boombox. "That's a lot of switches. What does what? I usually just connect to the Bluetooth in my car."

Kat dropped to her knees next to him and pushed his aside. "My dad had one of these. Not *exactly* like this, but me and my sister used to play his old tapes. You could hook up a microphone to it and sing along. It was fun."

She slapped a couple buttons. Turned a knob. Stood up and stepped back. All three of them jumped when music blasted from the speakers. A screeching blast of distorted noise.

Craig recognized the song. Knew somebody had set it up.

The Who was his mom's favorite band. She said Roger Daltrey was a fox. Ever since she was a little girl. Craig had looked at some of his pictures. Aging well for a man of his career, but not a fox to Craig. Maybe when he was younger.

"My Generation" filled the gym as Jeff filled the bottle with gas. Sat back to pull his shoe off. Then the sock. Pulled the shoe back on before stuffing the toe of the sock into the neck of the bottle. Stood with it held out to his side.

Craig stopped him before he could jump into the break in the bleachers. "What do we do?"

Jeff walked backward for a few steps as he grinned. "Give 'em something to shoot at?"

"Fuck off," Craig said, but he couldn't resist smiling back. Reached behind to find Kat's hand in his again. Pulled her back into the corner. Dropped down behind a jumble of folding chairs to wait.

"This is a stupid plan," he whispered.

Kat nodded. "How long do we have to wait?"

Craig rose up to peek at the double doors they had entered through. Looked at Jeff crouched in his hole. Holding the lighter at the ready under the hang of sodden sock.

"Where are they?"

Craig shrugged as he sat back. Held her against him as he waited. Eased to the edge to get another look at the gym.

"Craig?"

"What?"

"Something's up there."

Her hand floated up to point to the top of the bleachers on the other side of the gym. Into the dark space of the mezzanine.

At first, he only saw shadow, then the darkness moved. Rose up and became the shape of a man in a suit made of jungle. A bow with an arrow sticking out of it.

"Hey!" Kat shouted.

Craig threw his arm out to stop her, but she jumped out of hiding. Up and down with her hands waving.

The arrow burst into flames. Moved to aim at her.

Kat sprinted toward the trampoline in bounding strides. Leaped with a scream.

Craig saw the man draw his arrow. Reached out like he could save her with telekinesis.

Jeff stood with his arm back. Poised for the game-winning pass.

The arrow moved away from Kat to point at the new target.

Craig thought there was no way Jeff could possibly hit the guy from where he stood. Then he saw the bottle flying and wondered why he never lit it.

Kat hit the trampoline with a *whoop*.

The bottle shattered on the rail in front of the guy in the mezzanine.

The trampoline tore with the sound of a snapping steel cable.

The man above them exploded into a white spot of fire as the flaming arrow ignited the gas.

Kat plunged through the hole in the trampoline with a strangled scream.

As the man fell back, the arrow flew into the metal rafters. Bounced through the tangle to spiral down like a leaf. Trailing fire to the floor.

Jeff pumped his fist with a cry of triumph.

Craig shot from his hiding place, skidding to a stop next to the edge of the trampoline.

"Kat!"

He threw the mats aside. Gagged at the smell of the soaked stuffing. The revolting feel of the greasy canvas against his skin. He imagined her tromping through the rancid water collecting in the pit beneath the trampoline. Clawing at the wall to get out.

He stopped when he got to the apron. Bent his ear to the space between the rusting springs. Held his breath and listened.

He heard her. A whimpering moan.

"We'll get you. Hang on, Kat. I promise."

He popped up to his knees to find Jeff holding the lighter out. His face still flushed from the joy of his successful throw. Just like winning the big game.

Craig snatched the lighter. Dropped to his chest to thrust his arms through the springs. Held his breath again as he struck the wheel.

It lit on the first try, sending heat and soot up into his face. He squinted against the glare and held his arm away, careful to keep the flame off the underside of the trampoline material.

Her open eyes glittered like rolling marbles. Blood trickling from her mouth looked like liquid coal.

The rusty metal spike that had punched through the flesh under her chin was between her broken teeth. Like she held a metal egg in her mouth.

One arm dangled at her side. The other stretched out to another spike going through her wrist. It rocked back and forth. Spending the last of the energy she had imparted to it. Like she was waving goodbye.

Craig dropped the lighter. Heard it hiss in a splatter of fetid water.

He sat up and pulled his knees to his chest.

"What is it?" Jeff said.

Craig looked up at the flaming mess of the man in the mezzanine. Tearing the suit of leaves off of him as he flailed and screamed.

Craig shrugged as he continued to stare. "It was just like *Rambo*."

The man threw the burning suit aside, but his clothes and hair were on fire. Black smoke rose from him like it had when Mia had burned. His thighs hit the railing, and his body went over. Plummeted to the gym floor, landing in a brown puddle with the sound of a gunshot.

The only flame that remained on him was a small lick of fire on one leg struggling to remain lit. It finally went out with the same hiss that had extinguished the lighter.

Craig put his face between his knees and wept.

Kat was the only person who ever really knew him. They were going to do shit together in life, maybe get an apartment together, kick the world's ass together.

And now she was gone, as was whatever future they'd had in store.

Perhaps none of them would have a future after tonight.

Chapter Twenty-Two

The batteries weren't up to it. Roger Daltrey now sounded like a slow Tim Faust. Hitting those low notes like when Home Free won *The Sing-Off* on NBC.

Craig turned his back on the trampoline where his best friend would lie until someone someday found her for a proper burial. He promised himself that if, no ... when, he got out, he'd come back with the authorities for Kat.

He looked over at the smoking corpse of the killer, wished he could take his anger out on the man. He turned away, looked at the boombox as it wound down. Slower and softer until it ground to a halt and the small red light on the face faded.

"I'm sorry," Jeff said, approaching.

"What do you know about it?"

"About how much somebody means to somebody else? A lot."

Craig wiped his nose on his forearm. "Thanks."

Jeff knelt beside him. Put his hand on his shoulder. Removed it. Put it back. "We should go."

"Why?"

"What do you mean?"

Craig slapped Jeff's hand away. "What's the fucking point?"

"SHH!"

"Why? Let 'em come."

"What is wrong with you?"

"I'm done. I don't care if they find me."

His voice echoed back to him. Ragged and hoarse.

"Maybe I care if I get out. You ever think of that?"

Craig had to admit that he *hadn't* thought of that. He tucked his face back down. "Just leave me alone."

Footsteps behind them made him spin around. Spreading his hands like he was ready for a welcoming hug.

Embracing the death he knew was coming.

Instead of Ray carrying a butcher's knife, it was the hacker cradling a stuffy. She ran into the gym with it held against her chest. Eyes wide and excited.

She stumbled when she saw the smoking body crumpled on the floor. Veered wide before continuing on to stand looking down at Craig. "We have to get out of here."

Craig shook his head. "I don't want to win anymore. I don't think I ever did."

She turned her gaze up to Jeff. "What's he talking about?"

Jeff pointed at the hole in the trampoline. "His girlfriend died."

She blinked in confusion. "*Girlfriend?*"

"Jesus Christ!" Craig shouted. "You realize I'm gay, right?"

Jeff shrugged. "My sister has girlfriends. She's autistic and has cerebral palsy, but I don't think she's gay. How important is this right now?"

Craig put his head in his hands. "I don't know. I just don't know anymore."

"What's your name?" Jeff asked.

She pointed to Craig. "He never told you?"

"Nope."

She pursed her lips. "Fuck it. Schae Gardner."

"A hacker, huh?"

"Yeah. N0BLE is how I'm *really* known."

"In the Matrix?"

Schae snorted laughter. "Sure. Now, with that out of the way, can we please?" She dropped to her knees to look at Craig. "I'm sorry about your friend, but I remember what your *other* friend said about squad mode before you climbed through the window."

"Just go," Craig said. "I don't want to be a part of this anymore. I don't care about the money."

Jeff set the end of the bat down like he was leaning against a cane. "I do. Angel could have a good life with that money. Or a *better* life."

Craig had only thought about it in terms of what his mother wanted for him. A good school and a good future. The family could use that money. But then having money freed up by no longer having to save for college would help. He wasn't being selfish. He was just doing what he was told.

He waved them away. "Then go get it."

Schae rolled her eyes. "I already told you, there probably *isn't* any money. Besides, there's another way out."

She held the stuffy out. A little rabbit.

Craig looked into its button eyes. "I don't get it. Like some *Alice in Wonderland* shit?"

"Like drugs?" Jeff asked.

"What?" She shook her head and pulled the rabbit back into her embrace. "No. This is just a clue. I'm saying that you're forgetting the second rule your friend told you about. *Never stop moving.*"

She stood back up. Held her hand out for Craig. He looked, but didn't take it.

Then Jeff extended his hand too.

Craig sighed. Grabbed a hold of both offerings and let them lift him like a slip of paper. He was protected between them. Like they were shielding him from the paparazzi.

He thought of his own camera. The cameras of the others. Pulled his phone out. Swiped to the location screen. Three dots in a cluster. Two more so close to each other they were almost one spot of color. Selena and Marcy must have still been in each other's arms.

Telling themselves how pretty they were and how much they deserved the money over everybody else.

Craig swiped to the videos. Ira's feed was a trembling view of an empty room. Just a dying fire and a camp chair.

"He's gone."

Schae and Jeff crowded in to see his screen instead of using their own. Schae's curly hair blocked his view. "Who, Ira?"

"No, Ray. I don't see him anymore."

"Is he coming here?"

"I don't know."

Jeff lifted his bat. "Then let's remember rule two, right?"

Kat's face flooded his memory. No matter how hard Craig tried to remember her smile, it changed to the terrible seconds of her death with the metal shining from her mouth.

Her pleading moan.

He let them lead him toward the door, only to collide with Jeff's hip when they came to a skidding halt. Schae hissed in shock to take a step back, and Craig found himself exposed by their separation.

He looked over his shoulder in confusion. Saw her gaze fixed on the floor in dawning horror.

Instead of looking at what she saw, Craig looked at Jeff, only to find a similar expression filling his eyes.

With a defeated sigh, Craig looked down at his feet. Shifted his gaze along the floor until he saw it.

The oily stain on the floor where the killer's body had been. A haze of smoke hanging over it.

Jeff jumped like he'd been hit with an electric shock. Grabbed Craig's shoulder and steered him toward the door. Rushed into the hall with his bat held up and ready. Schae protested quietly behind them. "That's not the way."

Craig didn't bother correcting her. They were going to get Ira.

Past the double doors that the app on the KyMera phone told them was the auditorium. Craig resisted the urge to jump aside and try the handles.

The hallway continued deeper into the building. Shadows so dark anything could have been hiding inside them. Craig didn't know where they were in relation to where they had been on the floor above them when Ira had fallen through, but Jeff seemed to know where he was going.

He led them right to the door opening into the room Ira had fallen into. The stench of paint and chemicals. Piles of garbage and decaying carpet. Moss and black algae growing out of the cracks in the walls.

"Where is he?" Craig said, just as he realized it wasn't the room on Ira's video.

Jeff continued down the hall. "I don't know."

Schae pointed at a slight glow coming from a doorway farther down the hall. "Is that it?"

Of course. The campfire.

Jeff moved along the wall in a crouch with the bat held up in front of him. Craig didn't hold on, but he put his hand flat on Jeff's back. The muscles under his touch were like cables.

Schae held onto Craig's shirt tail. They were like a line of ducklings.

Over his own breath, Craig heard a voice. As they got to the edge of the doorway, he recognized it as the tune to the same song they had been playing on the boombox. Somebody else was a fan of The Who.

Jeff took a deep breath. Jumped to stand in front of the doorway with the bat held over his head. Craig followed to stand peeking out from behind his left hip. Schae jumped out to join him behind the right one.

Ray hadn't left the room. He had just stepped out of frame.

He looked up with a smile as Jeff settled into his stance. He held a small knife in a reverse grip. The rust-covered blade pointed at the floor. "Welcome, children."

He lunged at Ira and drove the knife into his throat. Craig jumped out with a scream. Schae pulled him back into the hall.

Ray jerked the knife free. An arc of blood followed the blade through the air.

Ray dropped into a crouch that matched Jeff's. Plunged the knife into Ira's just below his breastbone. Ira's howl was a gurgling screech of agony as Ray put his weight on the handle and pulled the blade down until it caught on Ira's waistband.

Ira's next scream increased the pressure in his abdomen, and his intestines swelled out of the weeping slit in his belly. A stretch of glistening skin holding it in a quivering mass as he took another bubbling breath. His third scream split the viscera with the sound of a tearing cloth, and his guts spilled out in a splatter of looping tissue and gore.

Craig's own scream filled his ears as Schae took a double handful of his shirt and dragged him away. Jeff's frame filled in the space behind him, and Craig turned to clutch at Schae's shoulders as his feet tried to keep him upright.

It wasn't until he felt rain on his face that he dared open his eyes again.

Chapter Twenty-Three

Ray never believed Wilkie was dead. Even when he saw the video from where Wilkie had staged his phone to catch him flying over the rail with fire trailing from what remained of his ghillie suit.

But even if he was gone, except for a swell of sadness, it hadn't really mattered. Ray's work continued.

The sound of that little one screaming down the hall. The nearly one and a half million people now online watching the Operation: Gen Z feed were probably going insane.

He lowered himself into his chair with a wincing groan. He needed some rest. His painkillers. Maybe a snort of whiskey.

He caught his breath as he wiped the blade on his pants. Smeared trails of thick blood, and the knife came away cleaner than how it had started.

He rolled up his sleeve. Dialed Grace's number, and while he waited for her to answer, he found a fresh bit of skin between the slices he had made in the dark of the coat room.

Dug deep just as her voice came over the speaker. "You watching this, babe?"

He breathed the pain out through gritted teeth. "Watching it? I was *doing* it."

She knew computers. Phones. *Technology*. Had a young body she was willing to give him. Wanted him and Wilkie to do things to her ... always asking for more. He believed masculine excellence included being respectful of a woman's desires.

Some of the things she asked for stretched that notion, but who was he to stand against what an independent female claimed she wanted?

"I'm sorry," she said. A meek sound just shy of a whine.

He made another slice. Found the strength to forgive her. "So, you're still on top of it?"

"Yes. The feed is going out like you wanted. Routed through TOR. KyMera and ..."

He ignored the rest of what she was saying in favor of concentrating on the sweet pain burning out of each cut. Distracting him from the cancer and the weakness and his own personal failings from long ago.

"Babe?"

"Yeah, I'm here."

"I think they found Eugene."

He leaned back with a grin. Closed the knife with a snap. "Good. And how are we on power?"

"The fence is live for another seven hours."

"That's good."

He tipped his head back and closed his eyes.

"Babe?"

"Yes, Grace?"

"Do you still love me?"

He grinned. "You tell me."

There was a pause. "I think you do."

She knew how to respect her elders. "Then you have your answer."

He hung up. Dialed Wilkie's number. Ignoring the phone when it brought up his name and image automatically. Ray preferred to type the number in manually.

His voice sounded raw when he answered. Out of breath. In pain. "Yeah."

Ray sighed. "What happened?"

Wilkie growled. "They got me with my own shit. Lured me in with a call and a decoy, and I fell for it."

"Proof that irony's not dead."

"Huh?"

Ray shook his head even thought there was nobody there to see it. "Are you injured?"

"Fuck yeah, I'm injured. I'm burned up, and I think I broke my shoulder. Tore up inside a little. Rung my bell pretty good."

"Can you continue?"

"Can *you*?"

Ray thought about it before answering. "I believe I must."

"Then you got your answer."

Ray threw his head back and laughed. Just as Wilkie's methods had been used against Ray, so had Ray's words been used against *him*.

He stood up and held the phone away from his face. "Get with Grace to see if she needs anything. Then see if she sees anything. There're still two birds in the nest upstairs. The others will come back soon enough, and I'm positive they'll have the old man with them."

It was funny for one old man to be calling the other one *old*. Still …

"Copy that," Wilkie said.

"Then report back to me in the auditorium.

Ray put the phone and the knife away. Walked over to Ira's body. Stripped off the body camera. Strapped it to his chair and aimed it at the dripping mess of Ira's hanging guts.

Let the kids look at that for the rest of the stream.

He took his time lighting another cigar. One last smoke to accompany his final hunt.

Chapter Twenty-Four

Craig held on as they stumbled through grass as tall as his shoulders. Sliding in the puddles. When they had passed by the gym, he'd flinched away from the open doors. There was too much out there in the open.

He couldn't hide from anything. Including the images of his dead friends burning like still-glowing ash in his mind.

Schae steered them into the darkness behind the building. Under the buzzing lines supplying power to the fence. Along the side of an old wood shed that smelled like metal and cedar.

Rain dripped from his bangs. Rolled down his back. His pants were soaked up to mid-thigh.

"The rabbit led me to him," Schae said.

Jeff looked over with a disbelieving sneer. "The stuffed bunny?"

Schae nodded. "It was a clue. Like he used to leave me. I found it in the wood shed, and it led me there."

She pointed toward a dark shape looming in the distance. Lightning flashed and turned the world into a blinding negative. Craig lowered his head in preparation, and the crack of thunder was like a board to his scalp.

He blinked the burning out of his eyes and let Schae's clawed grip pull him to what she had pointed at. A small structure of cubes with chicken-wire doors. The cubes on the bottom were large enough to hold a big dog. Or maybe a high-schooler.

Schae brought him to a stop. "It's a rabbit hutch."

Craig nodded. "Cool."

A rustling in the bushes, and Craig expected to see the very rabbits that were kept ... hutched? When the sound delivered a man coming out of the weeds with a reaching hand, he screamed and slapped at the air.

Jeff was the only thing keeping him from running away.

"Stop it!" Schae hissed. "It's my grandfather."

An old man. Taller than Jeff in spite of the stoop in his shoulders. White hair matted down like trampled cotton. Dark skin gray around his eyes and mouth. His patchy beard still had some color in it.

"Sorry about that. I had to hide still." His hand was still hanging in the air. "Name's Eugene, but everybody calls me Top."

Craig caught the hand in his in a habit that reared its head from deep within a remembered courtesy. "I'm Craig."

Top pumped his hand in a crushing grip. Let it go to direct it at Jeff. "And you, big boy?"

"I'm Jeff."

"Uh huh." Top wiped water from his eyes. Looked at Schae with a grin missing several teeth. "Alright, Sadie. Okay."

He dropped on all fours and crawled to the center door in the bottom row of cubes. Schae leaned over and whispered, "Sadie's my mom's name. He's just a little confused."

Top disappeared inside a cube that was suddenly even bigger than Craig had thought.

"It's okay," Schae said. "Trust me."

Craig shook his head. "I don't even know you."

"Fuck it," Jeff said, and he dropped down to follow Top through the rabbit hutch.

Craig's shoulders fell in defeat. Lightning blasted the color from everything, and this time the thunder was right on top of it. As if it pushed him down, he found himself crawling into the smell of fresh hay. A touch of vanilla.

He thought the light growing in front of him was what was left of the lightning making spots in his eyes, but it was a lantern. Warm and flickering as Top set it on a table.

"Get out of the way!" Schae shouted.

Craig rolled away and watched her emerge from the hole behind the hutch. Through a matching hole cut in a gray block wall. She turned to grab a board cut to fit over the entrance. Grunted with the effort of laying a bag of sand against it.

Sat back with a sigh. Smiled as she pushed dripping hair out of her eyes.

Top straightened from the lantern. "Don't get them phones out." He pointed to the ceiling. "That's how they track you."

They were inside a building of cinder blocks and concrete. As wet inside as it was out. Rusty valves and pipes on the far wall. A workbench scattered with food and tools. An old rocking chair.

Craig had no idea what the old man was pointing at. God? Aliens? "Where are we?"

Top looked down at him like it was the first time he'd seen him. "The pump house."

Craig nodded like it made sense. Stood up and put his hands in his back pockets. "Can you tell me what's going on?"

Top grinned. Looked over at Schae. "I was hoping you'd tell me."

Craig glanced at Jeff before looking at Schae. She shrugged. "I only know part of it. Top knows the rest of it, but …"

Craig held his hand up. "But he's confused."

She nodded.

"So what do we do? Hide in here until graduation?"

Top shook his head. "You can't hide for long."

"Then what?"

Schae moved up to the old man. Grabbed his arm. He smiled down at her. Touched her face like he had never seen anything lovelier. She took his hand in both of hers and looked up into his face.

"I found out where he was from his letters."

Top closed his eyes. "My Sadie."

Schae sighed and looked at the floor. "He came here after helping my sister take care of a problem. Something his talents were needed for."

Jeff set his bat on his shoulder. "And what are his talents?"

Top's eyes popped open. He took his hand from Schae's. Reached behind him and pulled a hatchet from a loop at his belt. "I provide all *kinds* of solutions."

Schae took a loud breath. "Top … My grandfather isn't well. He has dementia. A lot of what he told me in those letters I just didn't believe. But when he mentioned KyMera — a name a seventy-year-old hermit hiding from the government shouldn't really know much about — I looked into it. Found out most of what he said was real."

Craig wished he had a bat. Then he would have something to do with his hands. "Hiding from the government? Why? What was the problem your sister needed help with?"

Top dropped into his chair. Tapped the hatchet on his thigh as he rocked.

Schae crossed her arms. "None of your business."

"Fine."

"I just don't want to talk about it."

"*Okay*."

She sniffed before continuing. "He went here. Back before it was closed down in the sixties for the way the headmaster abused the boys. Cruel, *twisted* shit."

"He made us men," Top said as he tested the edge of the hatchet with his thumb.

Schae rubbed his shoulder. "He was being held here by a man named Ray Wardell."

"The bus driver?" Jeff shouted.

She nodded. "Yes. I don't know how. What he's holding over him. Or if he really even knows who my grandfather is."

Top smiled. His eyes glittered in the lantern light. "Oh, he knows me just fine."

Schae spread her hands. "So I came to get him out."

Craig held up a finger. "Wait. You really didn't come to win?"

She rolled her eyes. "I told you. There *is* no way to win."

"But Karen Beal herself was on the bus. You saw her. How could she just set something like this up? You're saying she's in on some crazy asshole's plan to kill a bunch of kids?"

"Why not?"

"Because it's insane. How is killing your target audience the thing that's gonna sell your fancy phones and cameras and shit?"

"So you really think you can just go in there and tap your phone to the plate and what? Confetti falls out of the air? Boys in spandex come out to Riverdance for you?"

Craig shrugged. "Not the most unpleasant prospect."

Jeff's snort of laughter almost ruined Craig's poker face.

Schae growled in frustration. "You can't get out that way. They'll kill you."

"Then how *do* we get out?"

Top stopped rocking. "Not that way. But I know how to get us out of here. Down past the trees. Through a gate where I got a car waiting."

Craig shook his head and took a step back. "No way. You said he had dementia. He calls you *Sadie*. We're gonna follow him to a gate in the rain in the *dark*."

She nodded. "And we'll have to turn the power off."

"How?"

"Go back inside to a control room."

"A control room?" Craig wanted to crawl back out into the rain.

"That's what Top calls it. It's where the zombie is."

Top chuckled. "She ain't really a zombie. Just a little gal dressed so. Likes it rough."

Schae covered her face. "Gross."

Jeff nodded. "Good for you, buddy."

Top started rocking again. Lips stretching into a satisfied smile.

Craig sagged in defeat. "Fine. Whatever you say. I don't even know how I got here."

Schae looked away. "I rigged the contest. Jackson High wasn't even going to be close to getting the views required to qualify, let alone win. Except for Jeff's videos about his sister. She's so sweet. I wouldn't be surprised if she could have eventually won with nothing but that smile."

Jeff lowered his head. "Thank you."

Craig laughed. "So I'm here because of *you*? I might die to some angry Boomer because you wanted to visit Grandpa Top here?"

"It's not like that."

"But it's *exactly* that. I'm here, and Kat and Ira are dead. Because of you."

When she said nothing to defend herself, Craig sat down on the floor. Pulled his legs up and rested his head on his knees. "Why would anyone want to kill kids?"

Schae hugged herself. "It's like some enforced stunt to drive traffic to a new website. Social media engagement like I've never seen."

"Cool, but that doesn't explain why Boomers hate us so much. It doesn't explain what we did that deserves this other than growing up in the world *they* created."

Top held the hatchet up in front of his eyes. "Children are now tyrants, not the servants of their households."

"And *that's* a reason to kill us?"

Top lowered the hatchet and shook his head. "Complaining about the next generation is just us missing our childhoods. Missing a more simple time. When I was your age, my grandfather used to say the same thing about us. Then we grew up and forgot about what it was like to get blamed for everything wrong with the world. We turned around and did it to you kids. Don't take it personal, son."

Craig shot to his feet. "Don't take it personal. Are you fucking kidding me? People are *dying*!"

Jeff pointed his bat at Craig. "Hang on. Let's just calm down." He turned to Top. "Craig lost his best friend and his ex. Murdered in front of him. Let's get him out of here."

Craig felt his control slip. Tears flooded his eyes, and he couldn't get his breath.

Top stood up. "I won't leave any other kids in there for Ray to feed on. We gotta go in to shut down the fence. Might as well get the others while we at it."

Craig wondered if Selena and Marcy would even let themselves be saved. If they weren't already dead.

Chapter Twenty-Five

Top took them back inside by a different route. Through an old metal door frozen shut with rust and old paint. Into the spray of a storm that had grown in the few minutes they had been hiding inside the pump house.

Craig imagined the night vision Ray would use to find them. Or the infrared. Body heat making them look like glowing gingerbread people.

Rain made his clothes hang heavy. Filled his eyes and poured into his mouth. The bulge of the phone in his back pocket was a needling feeling of awareness. He would have been cradling his personal phone. Fear building with every step.

Not just the money in losing an expensive device due to water damage, but he would lose his lifeline. The thing that kept him in touch with the thousands of people he had convinced himself were friends.

He didn't care about the KyMera phone, but there was still that tug at his attention. That anxiety that always accompanied carrying something like that.

He'd seen new mothers pay more attention to the

safety of their phones than the tiny humans balanced precariously in their laps.

Craig had no idea where they were. He felt the weight of Oakridge Academy hanging over them as they tracked along the base of a wall. The empty space to their left. The impression of sagging trees in every flash of lightning. The glitter of the metal fence back in the leaves and weeds.

Like a hundred staring eyes.

Top ushered them through a narrow opening between the edge of a sheet of plywood and the rotting door frame underneath. A dank hallway opening into a room of near complete darkness that smelled like spoiled cheese.

After only a few moments huddled together, Craig realized he could see. A line of dim light around the edges of a door several feet away. A washed-out vision of Jeff and Schae next to him. Top creeping deeper into the room with his ear cocked as if to listen.

Schae pulled her phone out and held the lit screen up. Top held his hand up to shield his eyes from it as he moved in a crouch to the door.

Glistening mud that looked like a giant slug trail covered the floor. Black mold and pale mushrooms down in the corners.

He waved them to follow. Craig grabbed a handful of Jeff's shirt. Moved his feet in step. Reached back for Schae and felt her fingers tighten over his. They stopped next to Top, and he bent to whisper, "She's right outside."

Jeff looked at the line of light around the door. "Who?"

"The zombie. Though she's more of a vampire by my experience."

Craig opened his mouth to shout. Let his air out in a frustrated hiss. Took a more measured breath. "What are you talking about?"

Top pointed at the door. "Grace. She's sitting in the AV room across from the auditorium just up the hallway here. Watching the cameras."

"What cameras? The ones from our phones?"

Top nodded. "And the ones installed all over the place."

Craig closed his eyes. He wanted to punch himself in the jaw. Of course they would have cameras. They had an electric fence. A fancy wireless network. Why wouldn't they be using other cameras?

He opened his eyes to see Jeff looking at him. Probably thinking the same thing. "Can they see us now?" Craig asked.

"No." Top shook his head. "And not even in the hallway outside. All the way to the windows of the control room. But once we get into the main hallway in front of the auditorium, they got us."

Schae sighed and stuffed her phone back in her pocket. "They can just track the phones anyway."

Top straightened with a smile. "Then why not throw them away?"

Craig looked from Jeff to Schae. Up to Top's knowing smile. Then he said what the others were afraid to. "Because what if it's real?"

"What? This place? The killing?"

Craig shook his head and looked away. "No. The money."

Top's remaining teeth shone out from his grin as he moved to stand between them and the door. Cracked it open with his eye to the widening gap. He pushed it all the way to the wall and stepped out into the harsh glow of video screens slicing through a haze of smoke and dust wafting by.

Without motioning for them to follow, he dropped into

a deep crouch and duck-walked to a row of windows set into the left-hand wall. Once there, he settled onto his knees. Craig could see the pain on his face.

Old joints.

Jeff dropped down to follow. Craig almost lost his balance. Recovered by dropping to all fours and crawling to keep up. Looked back to see Schae right behind him. He was grateful to be pressed back up against Jeff's back. Shivering against him as he tried to get rid of the chill of his saturated clothes.

Top eased up and looked through the window. Motioned for them to look. Craig imagined Scooby Doo's gang peeking around a corner in a neat stack of heads.

A woman sat in front of a bank of screens. Her back was to them, but Craig could see the wild hair and the blotchy skin. Tattered and filthy clothing. Grace and her zombie costume.

He couldn't blame Selena and Marcy. If she would have come at *him* with a knife, he would have probably peed himself.

Many of the screens were blank. Others had the static image of various Oakridge locations. Some were videos from active body cams. One showed a hand holding a burning cigar.

Grace put her phone to her ear. Cycled through the images in front of her. "Yeah, babe?"

Her voice was squeaky and nasal.

Craig had the urge to pull out his phone to see which monitor was his.

"I don't think it's working."

The sound of the storm was a constant blanket of white noise. He had to strain to hear what she was saying.

"It shows them pretty much in the room with me."

She turned in her chair, and they all dropped below the

bottom of the window. Scooby Doo and the gang hiding from the zombie.

Pesky kids.

"You can check for yourself, but there's nobody here. Maybe it's the rain or something."

Craig didn't want to be the first one to see if she turned back around.

"I wasn't being disrespectful, babe. I was just answering your question."

Top scooted backward. Head down like he was pulling something with his teeth.

"Yes, I *did* use sarcasm. I didn't mean it. I was just ... of course. I'm sorry. You can take it out on me later."

The sudden change in her voice made Craig shudder. The way she purred at whoever she was talking to. Probably Ray. He wouldn't be surprised if she started calling him *Daddy*.

He didn't stand up until they were back in the mushroom closet. He couldn't exactly call it *safe*, but he still sighed in relief when Top closed the door. He crossed his arms and edged closer to Jeff's body heat. "So, what now?"

Schae pulled her phone out. "We should leave these here. Just until we find Selena and Marcy. I think that's what she was talking about."

Craig couldn't make sense of what she had just said, but Jeff shook his head. "But she can still see us in the cameras. Do we go in somewhere else or what? Or keep the phones and try to use the live feeds to locate Selena and Marcy?" He pointed at Top. "He could probably identify where they are by looking at their surroundings right?"

Top sighed before pushing into the group. "I think my Sadie here can explain why I might not be able to do that. I'm not ... everything is different now. Not like it was in my mind. The way I remember it."

"But you got us in through here?"

Top raised his eyebrows. "This room ain't changed *location* all the sudden. But it don't look like it used to. None of this place does."

Craig held up his hand like he was calming a growling dog. "Okay, okay. So what do we do?"

Schae put her phone back in her pocket. "We have to get past Grace."

"No." Top shook his head. "We have to kill her. Then we won't *need* to get past her."

Craig's abs tightened into a shiver, but he couldn't think of anything to say.

Schae looked like she was trying not to throw up. "At least it would keep her from sending those old guys after us."

Maybe Top was right.

Chapter Twenty-Six

They made a hasty plan. One with more parts than Craig thought was necessary. Left their phones in a neat pile on the greasy floor before creeping back out into the control room's glow.

Top dropped to crawl with his teeth gritted in pain. Into a dark doorway across from the windows. Jeff scooted along the floor. Past the windows to hunker down in the dark on the other side of an intersection leading to a part of the building so dark, it might as well have been the edge of a canyon.

Craig stood up next to Schae. Tipped his head back to look into her eyes. He missed Mia. Somebody his size.

She took his hand in a fierce grip, and they both drew in a deep breath. Blew it into each other's faces. She returned his nervous chuckle. Then her grin faded as she turned to the door.

They walked into the hall, and instead of crawling under the windows, Craig fell against them like he was having trouble staying on his feet. Schae pretended to hold him up, but her scream when something slammed against the glass wasn't fake.

Craig tried to jump away, but Schae's weight kept him pressed against the window. He rolled his eyes up to see Grace with her face smashed on the other side. Leering mouth and wide eyes. He had to admire her commitment to the character.

Her scream was guttural. Saliva splattered out ahead of a creeping fog from her hot breath. Then she spun away with a huge knife held high over her head.

Craig dragged Schae back toward the door behind them as Grace rushed out of the control room. Sprinting toward the intersection with the knife still over her head. Tongue clenched between her teeth.

Grace rounded the corner, and even though Craig knew Jeff and Top were going to be there to save him, he still backpedaled in a panic. Schae holding him up as his feet churned. Or maybe he was holding *her* up.

Jeff lunged out of the dark, and his bat connected with a wet crack, burying into the meat between Grace's shoulder and neck. She dropped to her knees with a choked shout, and the knife flew from her hands.

Craig jumped as it skittered by, but Schae slammed her foot down, stopping it like stepping on a spinning dime.

Grace straightened with both hands digging at the pain in her shoulder. Mouth wide as she pulled in a deep breath to scream.

Top shuffled out with the hammer side of his hatchet swinging up from his knee to hit Grace on the point of her chin. Teeth shattered as her broken jaw slammed shut. Blood exploded from her torn lips, spraying into the air as her head whipped back.

Grace fell back to land flat with her arms extended above her head. Top grunted as he dropped his weight to his knees. Brought the hatchet down to bury the blade in Grace's throat.

When he pulled the hatchet free, a jet of crimson sprayed across the old man's chest. Craig turned away with his teeth clamped onto his tongue. A shrill hissing whine like a pressure relief valve full of steam, and he buried his face into Schae's shoulder.

Her nails dug into his back, and her squealing voice in his ear sounded just like his.

When Craig heard the hatchet strike a second time, he tried to run away, but Schae held him tight. Trembling against him like a spring about to push the jack-in-the-box through the lid.

Craig slid out from under her arms. It felt like he tried to fight it, but he still turned to look.

Top stood over Grace's body. Blood dripped from the hatchet like rain hitting dry grass. Top looked from Grace's slack face. Met Craig's gaze. "You gotta finish 'em quick. Like catching a fish. Put 'em out of their misery. Matheson taught us that." He looked away and pointed at Jeff. "Let's get her on out of the hallway, young man."

Jeff nodded. His bat clattered to the floor as he bent to grab one of Grace's wrists. Top grabbed the other, and they dragged her through a red smear into the adjoining hall Top had been hiding in.

Craig wondered how Jeff could be handling it so well, then he saw the mask of tears covering his face. The wide eyes. His mouth peeled back in a grimace of panic.

Craig didn't want to look at Schae. Did she feel like it was her fault? For rigging the contest and getting them into this?

She had no way of knowing there was a psychopath behind it all. A murderer who hated the younger generation. Livestreamed to hungry viewers.

Zoomers Vs Boomers. The pay-per-view of the century.

Craig put the heel of his hand in his mouth and bit down against the giggles that were tightening the muscles along his ribs. A terrible grin behind the pain.

Top came back and wiped the hatchet across the front of his shirt before hanging it back in its loop. Jeff crept past him and bent to grab the bat. Hugged it to his chest like a kid cuddling with a teddy bear.

Top looked around like he didn't know what he was looking at. Confusion in the way he held his hands out like he was trying to keep his balance. Then his gaze rose to look past Craig's shoulder. Top smiled. "Hello, Sadie."

Schae pushed out from behind Craig. Slid along the window as she walked toward Top. "What do we do now?"

Top looked down at the stripe of blood on the floor. It looked like oil. "We need to get ready for Ray to come calling."

Jeff nodded. "We need to go back to the gym. The rest of the gas."

Craig leaned against the wall and locked his knees so he wouldn't fall. Took a deep breath through his fingers before lowering his hand. "Another bottle from the ... whatever that room was?"

Jeff pulled his shoulders back. Breathed through his nose. "Yeah. It worked once."

"Not really. The guy got up."

"It'll work again."

"Fine."

Top flapped his hand like they were a bunch of chickens trying to get on his porch. "You kids go on. I'll get something ready for here."

Craig took the dismissal as an opportunity to get as far away from Top as he could. Back down the hall and into the fungi room. Before he could turn back to see if anybody was following him, he felt Schae's hand grab his upper arm.

Then Jeff's weight pushing them out the door into the rain.

Chapter Twenty-Seven

Ray threw the butt of his cigar into a puddle filling up with gritty rain water. He walked down the center of the hall toward the gym.

He heard an echo. A voice ... like a scream? The sound of the rain over everything made it hard to pinpoint either distance or direction.

He turned into the gym. Squinted into the darkness. Walked along the perimeter. Avoided the broken bleachers turning into wet sawdust. All the way around to the wide doorway where he paused to look around one last time before leaving.

He heard a noise above. Froze to tip his ear up. Heard it again. A rustling of fabric. A metallic click.

Ray spun out through the door. Down the hall to the stairs that led to the mezzanine. He took them two at a time until his hip popped, and he had to slow down. Limped up the last ones while hissing in pain with each step.

He stepped out of the stairwell and waved the haze of acrid smoke out of the air. Old gas and oil. Cooked meat.

He heard the noise again. Saw a ragged lump of greasy char roll over. Bright teeth bared in pain. Wilkie was on his back. A deep breath that caused him to choke on a phlegmy cough.

Ray rushed forward to work his way to his knees. Leaned over Willkie's body. Reached out. Drew his hands back. He didn't know where he could touch him that wouldn't cause him pain. "Why didn't you say anything?"

Wilkie's grin split the blackened skin at the corner of his lips to reveal streaks of pink flesh underneath. "I didn't want you to be disappointed."

Ray shook his head. "You did good enough, son."

Wilkie reached out and took Ray's hand. "Help me get to the rail over there. I'm busted up pretty good. Don't think I can make it."

"Why?"

"That's where my bow is. I can lean on the bottom rung there. Shoot any that comes by."

Wilkie was huge. Ray didn't know if he had it in him to drag his big ass the rest of the way, but he wasn't going to let him down by not trying.

The burns were hideous. Bits of the ghillie suit melted into his skin. Most of his scalp showing crispy fat. Bone showing through. One eye almost black with blood. His friend was dying, and even though they both knew Operation: Gen Z would end with them dead by the barrel of a cop's shotgun, this was sickening.

Zoomers getting the best of them. Wilkie failing him.

Ray shook his head. Pushed to his feet, ignoring the pain that radiated up from his hips into his lower back.

"No. You did this to yourself."

Wilkie shook his head. "Please. Don't be mad."

"I'm *not* mad. I'm just disappointed."

Wilkie's despair made more of his skin split open. Fluid

bursting from the surface of his burns as tears poured from his eyes.

Ray turned away. Didn't look back as he left the mezzanine. Hit the bottom of the stairs and took the short path through what used to be a narrow hallway and an equipment storage room. A shortcut to the control room where he emerged just down from the intersection in front of the wall of windows.

Paused when he saw something piled up near the end. Walked on his toes and breathed through his mouth. Slow and quiet until he could make out what it was.

Grace. Head hanging on by a strip of bloody skin.

He clamped his teeth shut. Moved to the end to peek around the corner. When he saw it was empty in every direction, he angled his toe to rub along her ankle as he stepped out into the open and moved to the control room door. Stepped inside to look at the monitors.

Sneered when he felt moisture on his cheeks.

When he heard a shuffling scrape in the hall, he turned with his hand dropping to the knife in his pocket. He wondered if Wilkie had somehow managed to follow him. Got himself ready to defend against a burned monster with a bow and arrow.

It was Eugene Gardner.

Ray took a step toward the door. Anger and instinct made him want to jump out with a cry of defiance. Instead, he walked backward until he was in the corner pressed up against a tall cabinet. In the deep shadows untouched by the light of the screens.

He watched Eugene unroll a spool of razor wire. Decided he would just sit and wait. If Top had been recruited by the kids, they would be coming back. Ray would kill them all then.

If not, Ray would kill Top first. *Then* the kids.

Either way, he'd make the old man pay for betraying him, Matheson, and the legacy of Oakridge Academy.

This time, he let his tears fall.

Chapter Twenty-Eight

By the time they got to the corner, the rain had dropped to a noisy drizzle. Big fat drops, sparse but heavy, falling with the sound of sizzling bacon.

Craig retraced their steps — minus the sidetrack to the rabbit hutch pump house. It seemed like a long way around to a room that only felt like a couple doors down from where they had been.

The rain stopped as they rounded the corner. Just the dripping, and the splash on their feet. Craig looked back over his shoulder. "It doesn't bother you? Me in the front leading?"

He had to do something to get his mind off of what it wouldn't stop showing him. Blood and gleaming bone and fire curling young flesh.

Jeff shrugged. "It just means you die first."

Schae made both hands into fists. Growled in frustration. "What's with you two? Like Maggie and the unibrow baby from across the street. Natural enemies. Yet you stuck together?"

Craig turned back to walk along the wall to the door

Schae had pulled them through what felt like hours ago. "You stick with who you know."

Jeff's hand was on his arm. Gentle yet firm as it pulled Craig to a halt. "Look," Jeff started before pausing and looking at the ground. "I don't mean to be a jerk or whatever. I don't even really know I'm doing it. I just ... I don't know. Sometimes a smile slips out. Or I say shit I don't mean. Just trying to keep my head down, you know?"

Craig moved out from under Jeff's touch. "Oh, I know alright. I've spent most of my life keeping my head down. What the hell would *you* know about keeping your head down?"

Schae spread her hands. "Is this really the time and place for this?"

Craig mimicked her frustration. "*You* started it. And then Jock Water Polo here wants to blame his bullshit on what?" He pointed at Jeff. "You afraid another cheerleader won't have anybody to throw her panties at?"

Jeff took a half step back. "Haven't you been through about twenty boyfriends this year? Why do you care who throws panties at me, which doesn't happen, by the way."

"Oh sure."

"Hey, you throw yourself at as many dudes as you want. I'm not like that."

Craig put his hands on his hips. "Like what?"

"Like you."

"The fuck is that supposed to mean?" Craig shouted.

Schae held her hands up, looked around in panic. "Shush! They might hear us!"

Craig ignored her. "You're just homophobic."

Jeff's confusion put Craig on his back foot. "What? No, I'm not a *total* asshole. It's more like I'm *Craig*phobic."

Craig's mouth fell open. He closed his eyes to concentrate on what he just heard. "I don't understand. Craigphobic?"

"You're kind of a lot."

"A lot of *what*?"

"A lot of Craig." Jeff sighed and laid his bat across his shoulder. "You know utterly who you are and who you want to be. The world is full of labels, and you're supposed to pick one and wear it proudly. But I don't know who I am like you do. Sometimes I feel like a non-person. The only labels I get are the ones that people like you give me. Jock. Homophobe. Bully. I'm none of those things, yet you're totally cool calling me whatever. Maybe if I was as sure of myself as you were, it wouldn't bother me as much."

Craig sagged against the wall. He cast his memory back. Tried to remember a single instant of Jeff pushing him. Calling him some disgusting slur. *Anything* other than hanging in the background and watching with a half smile. "You could have stopped it."

Jeff laughed. "Stopped what? Stopped your friends loving you? Stopped you graduating with honors? Stopped the number of views you get? The subscribers and engagement? Could I have kept you from knowing who you are?"

"Yeah, well, maybe I'm not as authentic as you think." Craig was suddenly tired. Keeping his emotions pushed down so he could function without coming unglued. Running from murderers without knowing what he was running *to*. "I was only here for the money, but I don't even want to go to college. I just don't have the courage to tell my mom. It was easier her knowing I was gay."

Schae snickered. "Probably cuz she already knew."

Craig nodded. "She actually did know. Or at least *really* suspected."

Jeff looked up like he was looking for a constellation. "I know one thing for sure. I love my sister more than anything in the whole world. She doesn't even know what a label is. She's just Angel. My sister. I don't want the money for college, I want it for her. So she can be taken care of for the rest of her life. It's the only thing that matters."

Craig thought about the little faces that would come into his room smiling first thing in the morning. Giggling and jumping on his bed to wake him up. Now just a few years younger than him and moving toward finding labels of their own. "You're a brother. Like me. See? We aren't that different after all."

Chapter Twenty-Nine

Ray watched Top run his wire. Listened to the old man muttering to himself. Like he was arguing with somebody that wasn't there.

A few years ago, he had thought they both shared the same vision. If they couldn't save Oakridge Academy from the government, at least they could save the ideals they learned there.

They were coming. No matter how many injunctions Ray had filed. The last penny he would ever earn on earth paid to lawyers in their incessant efforts to keep the development firm from tearing the old girl down.

He caressed the wall behind him. A wall that would be coming down in a week. Finally in the hands of a company that wanted to put up a self-storage facility. A new gas station on the corner of the property an eighth of a mile away.

Matheson's estate paying for damages to students without the vision to see his teachings through. Nothing left for the defense of the building and grounds. It broke

Ray's heart to see it fall so low. To the weeds and wild animals.

And Top felt the same way. Right up until he didn't.

He never agreed with Ray's hatred of the Zoomers. Or maybe his dementia erased it from his mind. He was good at terrorizing the agents that came snooping, though.

Surveyors from the county. State engineers. Anybody who came in any official capacity — even a few KyMera representatives. Until Ray took the time to actually talk to them.

That's when he found out why the name of Beal was so familiar. Karen Beal's father had been a student of Oakridge. Ray remembered him. A smart little redneck that spent as much time in the coat room as Ray himself.

Dead from Agent Orange exposure. Cancer in his bones.

As a personal favor to Ray. From one Oakridge Academy son to another. He would get his revenge on the generation that caused Oakridge to fall.

Top was too far gone by the time the plans were put in place. Living in whatever empty building he could hole up in as long as his memory held.

And now there he was fighting against his own ideals. In the very halls that had taught him.

Ray would no longer wait for the kids to come back. He would step out and slit Eugene's throat so they could come back and find him on the floor the same way he'd found Grace.

Before he could push off from the wall and draw his knife, he saw a shadow move in the hallway. Just above the bottom of the window.

He drew back and watched as a tuft of hair moved across his view. It hit the edge of the door, and Ray saw the tuft belonged to the black-haired girl that Grace had fought off. Walking like a burdened duck with her gaze fixed on Eugene's back. Half of a jagged cinder block held against her chest like she was keeping a baby warm.

A dozen small strips of tape held the swollen slices closed on one side of her face. The eye above almost closed by a puffy bruise.

Behind her crept the other one. For some reason, *her* name leapt into his mind. Marcy. The blonde hanger-on. She held a long splinter of wood in both hands. Like a piece of trim torn from a doorway.

Tiny flecks of paint coming off on her fingers like chalk.

Once they got to the other side of the door, the lead girl stood up. No sound, but her face twisted with the effort of lifting the block to her chest. Little flaps of blood-soaked tape flopped down as she struggled to get the block over her head.

Her scream was the wail of a wild animal. Screeching pressure on his ears.

Eugene jumped in alarm, spinning to bring his hatchet up. Eyes wide and toothless mouth open in a silent howl.

The block came down onto his stretched lips. A wet crunch, and he reeled back into his own line of razor wire.

Blood pumped from his flopping jaw to cover the front of his shirt. The block crashed to the floor, and Eugene's feet wrapped up in the trap he was setting.

The hatchet flew from his hands as his arms flew out for balance, and he fell into the wall to slide down in a tangled heap.

Marcy's jump carried her over a loop of wire, and she landed on Eugene's chest, her knees digging into his ribs with the sound of crunching leaves.

She worked her way down until she was straddling his thighs, then she drove her stake into his belly.

His breathless cry was like a kettle losing steam.

Marcy stood to fall back in the other girl's arms. *Selena!*

Ray almost snapped his fingers from suddenly remembering her name.

Selena and Marcy edged away from the razor wire. Cried into each other's necks. Selena's medical tape dangled under her gaping slashes. Blood and tears shining around the grisly wound.

"We did it."

Ray couldn't tell which one of them had spoken.

"We're the pretty ones."

"We *deserve* it."

"We were meant to win."

Their voices faded as they carried each other down the hall.

"We're the ones."

Ray waited until they were long gone. Moved out of his hiding place to inspect the damage. When he got to Eugene's feet, the old man was holding the hole in his belly. Dark blood oozed between his fingers. Breathing in tiny gasping sips through the mangled flesh of his lower jaw.

"It's a good thing you already lost most of your teeth," Ray said.

Eugene's eyes rolled and blinked. His gaze finally settled on Ray. He looked lost and confused.

Ray leaned in to grab the chunk of wood Marcy had dropped. Stepped over the wire to plant his foot on the old man's balls. Drove his weight down as Eugene thrashed.

Ray drove the board down to stab the splintered end into Eugene's neck under the flap of skin hanging from his chin. Jerked it free and stabbed it down into Eugene's open mouth. Then into his eye. Then the other.

His rage finally ignited. His grief making the deep pain in his hips and spine bleed away.

When he was done, he dropped the broken wood onto the raw meat of Eugene's face. Waited for the spike of pain running under his jaw to subside. Made his way back to the control room. Stood to examine the monitors.

Three bodies creeping into the gym. Two more picking their way through the debris in a hallway. The three kids left from their little survival group. Selena and Marcy coming to meet them.

With any luck, they'd kill each other.

Ray settled back into his hiding spot. Tipped his head back for a rest.

Not much fun in *that*, though.

Chapter Thirty

Halfway through the dark hall that would lead them to the gym, they heard the screams. Craig paused to listen, but he didn't hear them again. He looked back, and both Schae and Jeff shrugged.

He couldn't tell where it had come from. The gym? Somewhere else? Were they walking into a trap?

"This whole place is a trap," Schae whispered.

It was like she had read his mind. A shiver passed through him as he started back toward the gym. Past a set of stairs black with shadows.

At the door, he pressed against the wall and peeked around the jamb. It was so dark in there. He reached for the phone to use it as a light. Stopped when he imagined the beacon he'd make for anybody hunting them.

He resisted a growl of frustration. Crept in and kept close to the mound of rotting bleacher spilling into the floor. Avoided the trampoline. Tripped on the boombox and tumbled to the floor with a curse.

Thankful it was so dark. It helped hide his tears. He

rolled to the side to sit with his knees drawn up. Heard the crunching of glass. Threw himself to the side with a gasp.

He pulled the phone out of his back pocket, now a bent and cracked mess. Just a few pixels flickering with color.

Schae dropped down next to him. "It doesn't matter anyway."

She slid her phone out. Dropped it on the floor. Picked the boombox up with a grunt. Brought it down twice. When she set it back down, she swiped her hand across the remains of the KyMera phone. Shards of glass and sharp plastic. A weird smell of ozone and pecans.

Jeff hunkered down next to them. "I found the gas."

Craig looked away from the shattered phone to the red can in Jeff's lap. "Cool. We don't have the bottle, though."

"It doesn't matter. I still have the lighter. I say we go back to get Top. Soak the control room and set it on fire. Then we fuck off and wait for the fire department. Like, wait it out in the pump house."

Another voice made Craig's heart stutter. "Are you still *here?*"

He threw himself back with a gasp. Flinched when Schae's weight fell across his legs when she did the same thing.

Jeff stood as if expecting it.

Selena and Marcy walked into the gym. In the dark, it looked like the entire left side of Selena's face was gone. Like her teeth were stretched into a grin that went all the way to her ear.

As she got closer, Craig saw it was a dangling bandage that looked like bloody teeth. The weeping slice over it gaped open as she spoke. "I told you. We are going to win. And we just made it easier."

Something glittered in her hand as she lifted it in front

of her. A shard of glass. The edge glittered like it was encrusted with diamonds. Red plastic in her palm looked like drying blood.

It looked like she'd smashed her phone like Schae had. Kept one piece as a weapon. And she was holding it up like she intended to use it on them.

"What do you mean?" Jeff said as he backed away from Selena's menace.

Selena shrugged with one shoulder. "We got one. Killed him while he was riggin' up some trap with barbed wire."

Schae sat forward. "What?"

Marcy nodded. Held up a wooden pointer. It looked like half a pool cue. "Yeah. Some old Boomer that thought he was going to get us. But we got *him*."

Jeff set the gas behind him. Held his hands up. "Hang on a second."

Selena stomped her foot. "Don't you *dare* tell me what to do."

Schae shook her head. Covered her mouth with both hands. "Oh, God."

"Yeah," Marcy squealed. "This old black Boomer thought he was going to catch us? We caught *him* instead."

Her wild gaze stopped on Selena. Became transparent love.

Craig stood up, feeling even smaller than usual. "You stupid fuck."

Selena gasped.

"That's how we were going to get out. He was helping us get out. The *only* way out!"

Selena snarled. "The only way out? You tap the plate." She held up the shattered remains of her phone.

Craig pointed at it. "With that? It's gone, you idiot."

Marcy rushed forward. "She can share mine."

Selena's snarl turned to a sweet smile. "That's right. Because we are supposed to win. We're the pretty ones."

Marcy closed her eyes. "Pretty ones," she breathed.

Craig threw his hands up. "He wasn't one of the bad guys."

Schae's sobs were pathetic breaths of agony behind him. He wanted to go to her and tell her it was going to be okay, but not only did he not believe it, he didn't want to take his eyes off of Selena's hands.

Selena pushed Marcy away with a sneer of disgust. Steadied the sharp point of her broken phone at Craig's chest. "I can't believe you. You're just too scared to do what you need to do to win. To *really* get out of here."

She took a menacing step.

"You're so weak, Craig. Unable to do what needs doing. Having a foot in every camp. So busy being the nice guy. Being the victim."

Another step, and Jeff moved in between them. Craig wanted to tell him he didn't need his protection, but he had to admit seeing Selena take a step back in fear was pretty satisfying. She leaned out past Jeff's wide shoulders to keep looking at Craig. "You don't have what it takes. You never did, and that's why my channel is five times the size of yours. You have to be aggressive."

She lunged past Jeff with her broken phone extended in front of her, but Jeff slapped it out of her hand.

Selena stood still with offended shock as her only expression. Looked up into Jeff's face as fresh tears spilled from her eyes. "Ow."

The arrow buzzed through the silence. It hit Selena in the side of the head, and the arrowhead burst out of the bone beneath her mangled cheek.

The impact knocked her a step to the side, and her legs

moved to keep her upright. Like a baby deer trying to escape the tall grass.

Marcy screamed. Put a hand on either side of her face just like the painting.

The second arrow punched through her open mouth, and she jumped forward like she was trying to catch the blood that burst out like red vomit.

She fell on her face with her ass sticking up. Arms spread out. Knees pressed together.

Selena's body finally got the message, and she dropped to the floor like she was trying to sit on her feet.

Jeff bent to grab the gas can. Took off in a crouching run. An arrow bounced off the floor in front of his feet. Thunked into the soft wood of the bleachers.

Craig pulled Schae to her feet and pulled her into a staggering jog.

The next arrow stuck in the floor.

Craig followed the angle of the shaft to a blank mass sitting in the balcony above them. Jeff had set him on fire. He'd fallen over the railing.

Now he wanted revenge.

Chapter Thirty-One

Craig tucked his head down and pulled. If he wasn't careful, Schae would overtake him, and he'd be bringing up the rear. End up the last one in the gym with an arrow up his ass.

Jeff ran through the doors at full speed, only slowing when he crashed into the wall across the hall. Craig and Schae were neck-and-neck when they passed through. An arrow banged off the door frame. Bounced in front of his face and stuck in the wall a foot from where Jeff stood panting.

Their feet sounded like Fred Flintstone trying to accelerate on a wet road. Craig took off down the hall, but he skidded to a halt with the realization that Jeff wasn't behind them.

Schae looked like she wasn't aware of what was happening around them. Her muscles were rigid, and she stood wherever Craig left her. Snot and tears shining on her dark cheeks and upper lip.

Craig heard Jeff's footsteps echoing in the stairwell. Jumped through the door to look at Jeff's silhouette climbing into the darkness. A dim rectangle of light above him at the top of the stairs.

He followed without thinking. Running with his head down and his arms pumping. Before the top, he ran into something. Bit his tongue as he bounced back in pained surprise.

Jeff's hand shot out and grabbed the front of his shirt. Two buttons popped off, and the seams under his arms strained like the cloth was going to rip to shreds.

Jeff dragged him back to safety and pushed him against the wall. Craig slapped his hand away. Instead of thanking him, he demanded in a harsh whisper, "What the hell are you doing?"

Jeff smiled. Barely out of breath after all that running. He held up the gas can. "I'm gonna finish the job."

"How?"

"He's gotta know we're here. I'm just gonna pop my head out—"

"And get it shot off, you dumbass?"

Jeff's smile was pinched around his eyes. "I won't. I'll pull it back in real quick. He'll fire, but it'll be too late. Then, while he reloads, I'll toss the can at him so it spills and I'll light it up. He won't have time to get another one going unless he's Legolas."

"That's the dumbest plan I've ever heard."

Jeff's smile became a grin. He reached into his back pocket. Frowned as he came out with his phone. "Hold this."

He handed the phone to Craig.

Then his grin was back after reaching back into his pocket and pulling out the lighter.

Before he could turn around and stick his head into the mezzanine, Craig slid his phone into his own back pocket. Grabbed Jeff in an embrace. "I'm sorry."

Jeff hugged him back. Craig squeezed his eyes shut. What a terrible way to live out a fantasy.

"Me too," Jeff said.

Craig stepped back to give him room.

Jeff nodded. Turned around to get a deep breath. Held the can up in one hand. The lighter up in the other. "Hey!" he yelled, then he darted his head forward and back like a bird poking its beak into a tree for a grub.

Just like he said, an arrow whizzed right by, digging into the wall just inside the door. Jeff didn't give a battle cry. No last words. He just threw himself through the door with the gas can in front of him as he hooked around the doorway.

Just before he tensed to lift it, an arrow appeared, sticking out of the side of the red plastic like magic.

Jeff stumbled back with a grunt. The arrow had gone all the way through. Deep into his ribs.

Craig thought Jeff was peeing himself until he smelled the gas pooling at his feet.

Jeff looked down at the dribbling gas can fixed to his side with a shaft of wood. When his mouth fell open, Craig saw blood in his teeth.

Jeff looked up and met Craig's eyes. Smiled as he held up the lighter with a slight shrug.

Craig threw his hands out with a wordless shout of horror as Jeff struck the wheel.

A tiny spark as he took his first step. A blue flame as his second step landed. A whoosh of flames that sent heat back that licked at the tips of Craig's fingers.

The bowman on the floor looked up from where he leaned against the mezzanine railing. It was as if Craig could only see his eyes. Wider than the whole world as terror gripped him. Staring at the sprinting flames coming for him.

Another arrow pulled back, but it was too late. Jeff was already falling on top of him by the time he let it fly. Burning gas spilling out like white lava.

Two voices combined in agony rose up from the thrashing pile, and Craig threw himself back into the stairwell. His heel hit nothing but air, and he tipped backward with the empty darkness behind him. Into Schae's arms.

She wrapped him up and steered him into the wall where the railing dug into his ribs. He clung to the metal to keep from pulling her down, then dragged himself to the next step while she asked what was going on in his ear over and over.

By the time they reached the bottom, she had stopped asking, and Jeff was no longer screaming.

Craig pulled her along in a daze. Both of them breaking the silence with only their labored breathing.

Through a narrow hall full of garbage. A dark room filled with more piles of soaking and stinking filth. Then even more halls with imagined terrors behind every corner.

He stopped to get his bearings again, glancing at a dark mound next to his feet. The crumpled body of the zombie. He had to think to remember her name. *Grace*.

He noticed the blood from the sickening stump of her neck had spread so far, he was standing in it. He looked over at Schae. Felt her trembling, so he put his arm around her. Pulled her away from Grace's body into the hall.

When he saw Top lying in the middle of tangled coils of razor wire, he turned until he was between him and Schae. Shielded her from seeing it until they were past it. "No. Don't ... don't look."

Led her into the control room where he eased her down into the only seat.

Leaned over her to put his hands on her shoulder while looking into the different screens.

Various cameras from all over the building. Empty halls. No movement except for the creep of black smoke floating over the gym like morning fog.

Only two phone cameras had an active video. Marcy's feed showed the dark metal rafters swallowing the background. The left half of the screen dominated by a close-up of her face. Bloated in death with an arrow protruding from her blue lips, bending under the weight of her body.

The other one was Jeff's phone. Nothing but a black screen. The edges brightening with color as Craig moved. Comments flying by the bottom that he refused to read.

There were over five million active viewers.

He pulled the phone from his pocket, and the room flared with light. He took a breath so he could scream into the camera at all the people wasting their time watching this garbage instead of living their life, then he sagged in defeat.

Slid the phone back into his pocket, turning the screen black once more.

He could see himself standing behind Schae in the reflection. Then another shape rose behind him.

Pain blossomed in the back of his head. He felt Schae's shoulders under his clutching fingers. Then he felt the floor against his cheek. Rough hands under his armpits.

He thought he heard a scream. A deep voice murmuring into his ear. Then he heard nothing. Relaxed into it as his own screen went dark.

Chapter Thirty-Two

Pain woke him up. His head throbbing. Sharp biting at his wrists. Numb fingers feeling like his hands were inside burning mittens. Above his head with his shoulders screaming with every deep breath.

Lights overhead shined down on him.

A bubbling wheeze through his nose. Mouth covered in duct tape, a corner flapping in his periphery.

He lifted his head. Winced as a wave of nausea made his knees weak, bringing more pain into his wrists as his weight drew him down.

He locked his knees and slowed his breathing. Looked up to see his hands bound with some of Top's razor wire. His fingers were swollen. Turning purple. Blood ran down his arms in lazy red rivulets.

He let his head fall forward. Looked sideways to find Schae standing next to him in the same predicament. Eyes wide and staring straight ahead. She shook as if voltage was passing through her. Sobbing behind the gag of gray tape.

Craig faced forward, but he didn't really want to look.

Keeping his eyes on the floor until curiosity forced his head up again.

He stood on a small stage looking out over an auditorium. He jerked in surprise when he saw the tap plate at the edge of the front row. A golden glowing square of flashing LEDs on a pedestal with the KyMera logo wrapped around it like graffiti.

It was real after all? His smile stretched the adhesive into a pinching around his mouth. Then he saw who was in the audience.

The bodies of the other kids from Jackson High. Lined up and arranged as if they were waiting for the show to start. Broken, burned, and bloody.

Craig felt like he was being judged. Like they were waiting to comment on his performance. Like when the keyboard warriors waited for his next video just to call him names in a DM.

Footsteps vibrated through the floor, and a shadow stretched out as Ray stepped in between him and Schae. He held a KyMera phone up in front of him. "And so we come to it, children. And yes, I am reading the comments. Wondering how we did it. Wondering who will win."

He put his back to the audience. Turned the phone to put Craig and Schae into frame. He looked at Craig. "You have become the favorite. I have to admit that I am surprised, what with all the talk lately of how women should be represented, but then I noticed in another comment that you were gay, and it suddenly made sense."

The razor wire jangled like jewelry when Craig shook his head. What the hell did he mean by him being gay made sense?

Ray sent his attention toward Schae. "It looks like you have been chosen ... not to win, but to be next."

Schae began kicking. Squealing into her gag as Ray came closer.

"I understand," Ray said. "But I have to do what the viewers want. Isn't that what your generation believes? Anything for the *clicks*."

The last was said with a sneer.

Then Ray grinned as he moved between them like a snake slithering through the rocks. Craig stood on his tiptoes to get enough slack to look behind him.

Ray had set up a blackboard behind them. Staged for the dead crowd to see.

CHILDREN SHOULD BE SEEN AND NOT HEARD.

Ray had written it in blue chalk.

He reached above him and grabbed a rope hanging from scaffolding over the curtain. Craig saw a noose in one hand and the frayed end in the other. He walked back to the front of the stage, and the sound of a pulley above them screeched as it moved along a track.

Ray let the end of the rope and the noose hang over the KyMera tap plate pedestal. Walked back between them to position the phone in the chalk trough of the blackboard so it could see the action.

When he positioned himself in front of Schae, she pulled away. Lifted a foot to kick. Ray caught it. Leaned in and punched her in the stomach.

When Craig flinched away from the savagery of the blow, his right hand slipped out of the loop of razor wire holding him to the hook. He stared at his bloody hand in wonder, but just before Ray turned to look at him, he shot his hand back up to grab onto the hook.

Ray stared for a moment, then back to Schae who was curled up and gagging into the duct tape. Fresh blood pouring down from where the razor wire was cutting into her wrists and hands.

"Let me help you," Ray said. His voice was gentle. Like he actually cared.

He jumped forward and grabbed her with his powerful hands just above her elbows. Lifted her off the hook like she weighed nothing at all. Slung her to the edge of the stage where she threw her hands out in front of her to keep from falling into the audience.

Ray calmly grabbed the noose. Tossed it over her head and pulled on the frayed end before Schae could duck out from under it.

She rose from the stage to hang out over the tap plate with her feet kicking like she was trying to run away. A choked hum came from her nose. Cheeks puffing in and out as she struggled for air.

Craig pulled his hand down. Pulled on the other, but the wire was caught on the hook.

Ray bent to the rope, and Schae rose another foot. Ray got a fresh grip. Tensed to pull again.

Craig screamed into the duct tape before snatching his left hand down with all his strength. The razor wire bit into him with wet blinding pain, but the wire came free of the hook, and Craig was crying over the bleeding mess of his left wrist and forearm as he stumbled toward Ray.

Schae went up another foot, and her feet slowed. Her face was swollen and blue.

Craig jumped up on Ray's back. Looped the dangling razor wire over his head. Grabbed the flapping end with his free hand and pulled it back into Ray's neck as hard as he could.

Ray let go of the rope to reach up for the wire digging into his throat, and Schae dropped to hit the tap plate with her heels.

The pedestal crumbled and the tap plate shattered as it hit the floor. Schae rolled away to end up lying in the shadow of the stage.

Ray spun in a tight circle, and Craig's legs flew out behind him. The razor wire cut into his palm. Deep into his wrist. Ray choked through the pressure. Clawed at the wire as his feet tangled, and he fell to his knees.

He threw himself forward, and Craig flew over his shoulder. Into the air between the stage and the front row.

Craig landed on the back of his head and the tops of his shoulders. Looking up into the stage lights. Ray blotted out the light as he tumbled over the edge.

Ray's weight crushed the air out of Craig's chest. He struggled to get out from under him, but Ray kept pushing him back down as he tried to sit up.

Craig tossed his left hand up to whip Ray in the face with the razor wire. Ray batted it away. Sent an elbow behind him that connected with Craig's eyebrow in a blinding flash of sound and pain.

Craig's head dropped back to crack on the floor. He looked up through a haze of confusion as Schae stood over them.

She held a long shard of glass from the tap plate in her hand. Blood soaked her arms from her wrists to her elbows. Poured from the fresh gashes in her fingers.

Her duct tape gag flopped over to reveal her teeth bared in a snarl. She jumped forward and brought the point of the shard down to sink into Ray's left eye.

Her weight bore him down to smack his head off Craig's shoulder. Her snarl became a feral growl, and she worked her way back up to her feet. Ray pawed at the glass sticking out of his eye, but before he could get it out, Schae lifted her foot up and stomped with a scream, driving the glass deep into his skull.

Ray tensed as his body spread out in a single spasm like he was holding onto the fence outside.

Then he sagged. Turned his head to cough blood into Craig's face. Took a hitching breath. Let out in a moan.

It was several seconds before Craig realized Ray was dead. "Get him off me."

Schae pulled just enough of his weight off for Craig to get out from under him. He kept his gaze on the floor in front of him so he wouldn't have to look at the other kids. Or Ray.

The flashing glow of the tap plate caught his eye. Still working even though it was smashed. He finally looked up to see Schae staring at him.

He worked his hand into his back pocket. Pulled out Jeff's phone.

The video feed was going strong. Comments scrolling along the bottom faster than Craig could read.

The view count was up to over six million.

He held the camera up so they could get a good look at his face. He knew *he* didn't want to see it. "Jeff was still trying to figure out who he was. How weird is that? I'm not sure I understand, but I know he didn't give in and just accept who the Boomers — or *anyone* — told him he was supposed to be. So never let other people define you. And when you figure out who you are, never apologize for it."

He let the phone fall to his thigh. Took a step toward the tap plate before lifting it back up. "Oh yeah. Get the fuck off this livestream and go live your lives."

He dropped the phone on the broken plate, and the light went from pulsing gold to solid green.

It looked like he wasn't the favorite after all.

Jeff won.

Six Months Later

Craig took another sip of his coffee. He'd had trouble kicking the narcotics after the surgeries. Add in the antidepressants that did little for his nightmares and anxiety, and he had decided he needed *something*.

Caffeine was his new drug. He liked coffee well enough before, but he had taken it to a new level since ... He just liked the fluttery feeling it gave him. The collapse of exhaustion when he finally went to sleep after thirty or so hours of being awake and wired.

He sat at a table outside the Hill of Beans. Watching the light filter in through the leaves as they turned the colors of harvest. He pulled his hoodie up against the cool breeze.

He still didn't have any feeling in his left hand. A hard brace tightened over it to keep his fingers straight.

When Schae came around the corner in a fall of bouncing afro, he saw that she wasn't much better off. Full cast on one hand with just her fingertips sticking out. A heavy glove on the other held on with padded Velcro.

She leaned in and kissed his cheek before sitting down. She smelled like apples and hand sanitizer.

He slid her cup to her. "I got you a large Night Owl with sweet cream."

She smiled as she took a sip. "You remembered."

He shrugged. "Well, it's what I drink now too, so …"

She closed her eyes and breathed in the steam coming through the little drink hole. "How are you?"

"Just peachy."

She sighed. "I don't have anything to report."

"What do you mean, report? This isn't an assignment. Just something you took upon yourself."

"I know. I just … Even if my hands worked, I don't think I'd find anything."

He knew there was nothing *to* find. KyMera had covered every angle. The blame had fallen on Ray and his cohorts. Even Eugene Gardner was blamed. Craig's and Schae's voices went unheard as they screamed their protest, and then they were silenced for good when the money came in.

Karen Beal wanted to prove how terrible she felt that her equipment had been used in such a horrible manner. According to the rules, they both would win. Plus a special prize to honor Jeff's sacrifice. Especially since they had used *his* phone to tap the plate.

Three million dollars. The exact amount of money it took to shut them up.

Craig took another sip. "You know, I've barely been online since? I haven't looked at a single LiveLyfe post or video. I think I'm done."

Her eyes glistened with unshed tears. "I can't. I need to know."

He shrugged. "Just don't go too far. You have people

you love who are easy to get to. I have my sisters and my mom. And I met someone."

Her eyes widened in genuine excitement. "You did? How?"

"Just a boy from rehab. A nice guy who doesn't know me from the fucking internet."

"That's great."

And it was. Jacob was loving but not clingy. Sensitive and caring. Assured of his place in the world, and when Craig told him how much he loved him, Jacob had said it back. Held him as he cried for hours.

And he looked a little like Jeff.

Craig was suddenly tired. Schae was the last thing in his life that kept reminding him of what he'd been through. He had started to take classes so he could eventually be able to help other trauma victims. Especially anybody in the LGBTQ+ community that suffered from abuse or PTSD or even just a touch of anxiety because they lived in a world that refused to accept them.

He stood up and tossed his cup into the trash. It still had hot coffee in it. Before he could look at the confused hurt he knew he would see on her face, he was distracted by a couple of teens walking along the sidewalk.

Both chatting, but not to each other. They wore the latest models of wearable streaming gear from KyMera. Talking to an invisible audience.

Craig looked down to see Schae had seen them too. As they walked by, she looked up at him, and the tears finally started falling.

Craig shook his head. "I just can't anymore, Schae. I'm going to move on. So should you."

He turned without another word. Not exactly how the meeting was supposed to go. But he felt lighter. A sense of peace and relief descending the farther he got away from her.

He got into the car and looked over at his own phone. Just a basic model that his mother had insisted he get. Another weight around his neck. His hand crept over to pick it up. Like it had a mind of its own and needed to be filled with the black plastic of a virtual world.

He picked up the phone. Opened the door and let it slip to the ground.

He felt the tire crunch over it as he pulled away. Wondered how long it would be *this* time before he bought another one.

He was no longer sure who was winning. The Zoomers or the Boomers. Thought about the millions of people who sat and watched Ray's murderous stream. Fell into the conspiracies that followed. Messaged him about how he should spend KyMera's money.

He'd even heard that Angel's page had over two million followers.

By the time he got to his first turn, he knew the answer. Nobody won.

They were *all* lost.

DON'T FORGET to like and subscribe.

What To Read Next

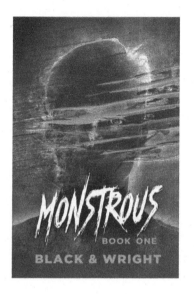

Is justice worth the price of your soul?

Henry Black finally had a loving family and a thriving career, until it was ripped away when three men murdered his daughter, and ended his world. Now he has a chance for vengeance.

GET MONSTROUS TODAY

A Note from the Author

Thanks for reading *Zoomers vs Boomers*

If you enjoyed this book, please consider writing a review of it on your favorite bookseller so other readers might enjoy it too. Just a couple of sentences would mean a lot to me.

Thank you!
Sawyer

About the Author

Sawyer Black writes dark and violent fiction for people who secretly love puppies and rainbows. In addition to being a U.S. Army veteran, he's also a beardsman. In fact, that's where all his ideas come from. The beard. Speculative stories about struggle and triumph and brutal emotion, written mostly for his ideal reader, his wife of nearly twenty-five years. He's an independent woman who likes cigars and margaritas, and he holds the deep belief that the earth is round.

CPSIA information can be obtained
at www.ICGtesting.com
Printed in the USA
LVHW091828230123
737779LV00012B/175

9 781629 551876